PUFFIN BOOKS

Editor : Kaye Webb

PS 207

THE BLACK SYMBOL

This is one of the most exciting stories we have ever published in Puffins.

It is set in Montana, at the time of the great American gold rush. The two heroes are twelve-year-old Barney, journeying across the desolate country looking for his father, and Steve, the great blind Negro, whom he finds imprisoned in a travelling medicine show.

It takes Barney a long time to realize that 'Doc' Cathcart is not the benevolent friend he first pretends to be, and by that time he also is a prisoner, with the Doctor showing documents to prove he is Barney's legal guardian. Together the two friends are forced to help the Doctor with his fraudulent show, until Steve with great unselfishness helps Barney get away.

The extra quality of this book lies in the absolute reality of the characters and of all the details that go to make up the day-to-day life of the wandering show. The authors are inspired story-tellers, and once you have started reading you will find you can't stop until you have reached the end.

For boys and girls of nine onwards.

The Black Symbol

Annabel and Edgar Johnson

ILLUSTRATED BY BRIAN SAUNDERS

PENGUIN BOOKS

Penguin Books Ltd, Harmondsworth, Middlesex
AUSTRALIA: Penguin Books Pty Ltd, 762 Whitehorse Road,
Mitcham, Victoria

First published in the U.S.A. 1959
Published in Great Britain by the Brockhampton Press 1960
Published in Puffin Books 1964

Made and printed in Great Britain by
Cox & Wyman Ltd, London, Fakenham and Reading
Set in Monotype Plantin

Contents

To Lewis Andersen
a fellow-questioner

PART ONE *The Bally*

In the first place, the word was 'ballyhoo', but the carnival men shortened it to 'bally' – the part of the Show that's performed out in front of the tent to draw a crowd

1

IT snowed the first week in June. The wind brought the storm blasting down out of the north as if it had been poured from a barrel. All day it slanted along the Beaverhead Valley in sheets, piling up drifts in the low places, leaving the ridges bare and clean. It wasn't very cold, but a man couldn't see as far as his horse's ears, so the big round-up had to be put off.

By nightfall, in the homesteads along the Valley, folks were beginning to fret. In one of the ranches shouldered down in the drifts of snow, everybody had finished supper early, grumbling about the weather. Hoping to get out and in the saddle at the first crack of dawn, the men took their lanterns and headed off to bed. One by one, the lights spread out through the old ranch house, while across the dooryard, in the lean-to by the barn, a boy stood and watched.

He had put his lantern on the floor beside the bunk so it wouldn't show from the window. It cast just enough light to make odd shadows on the clinked log walls of the narrow room where he slept alone. Only two years he had lived here on the ranch, but it seemed like most of his life. And now that it was almost over, this draughty little shed of his was the only place he would miss.

A sharp gust of wind screamed round the corner of the building, and Barney shivered. He was a slight-built boy, dark-haired, and not very tall. Most people put him down as eleven or twelve until he looked at them with that steady thoughtfulness that made him seem older. Now his face was sober as he listened to the wind. But it couldn't be helped – snow or no snow, it had to be tonight.

Even after the last light went out in the main house, he hesitated. No telling about the older people; they seemed to have a built-in sense of suspicion, although there was no way they could guess what he was going to do. He hadn't even known himself until this afternoon, when he'd heard Uncle George and Aunt Norah talking. They'd forgotten they had sent him down-cellar to sprout the potatoes, and when they'd got to discussing him up there in the kitchen he couldn't help hearing every word. And a good thing, too, or he'd never have learned that, come the end of the drive, they were planning to send him back east on the same train with the cattle. And do it without his father's even knowing it.

Barney swallowed hard against the fear that kept trying to shove up into his throat when he thought about his dad. Ever since the two of them had come west together, he had felt closer to his father than he ever had back home, when his dad had been gone all day, down in the coal mines. On the long trip they'd got to understand each other, and now Barney just wouldn't believe that his father was dead. It was true it had been almost a year since they'd heard from him, but Barney shut his mind to that and kept holding hard to the memory of his dad's face that day he'd left. John Morgan was a wiry Welshman with the same dark hair, the same humour and keen look that Barney himself was beginning to take on. Neither of them bore any likeness to Uncle George's side of the family, who were all blond, beefy six-footers. They had badgered his father about it being a chancy thing for an Easterner to head off into rough country, gold-hunting. They'd warned him that Alder Gulch was still a rip-snorting lawless place, but John Morgan had grinned at them confidently.

'I reckon I can play whatever cards get dealt,' he had said. 'Just take care of my boy for a while, and I'm going to bring back a sack of gold for each one of you.' And to Barney he'd spoken privately. 'It won't be long, Buz. I'll come back for you as soon as I can.'

Turning back into the shed now, the boy put on his heavy sheep-lined Mackinaw and a cap with ear-flaps. He'd greased his boots to keep the wet out, packed up a little food from the kitchen. He tried to think what else he would need. Uncle George and the boys were always blowing hard about the Morgan gumption and the Morgan muscle and the Morgan horse sense, all of which they made clear he had none of. Well, there wasn't any point fooling himself – Barney knew he was just as scrubby and small as they said he was. He did think he had more sense than they gave him credit for, but whether it was enough, he couldn't know until he'd tried himself out against problems.

He felt in his pocket – just to touch the little packet of his father's letters made him feel firmer inside. Dad was never one to run away from things, but he had hated the dark-smelling house back in Pittsburgh almost as much as Barney had. After Barney's mother had died they'd kept away from there, but he could still remember it, set on a steep hill, slam-up against the other houses, blinds always drawn, crochet work pinned all over the furniture. And his mother's kin were always proper and pinch-nosed. If he were ever sent back there, he thought, he might never see his father again – not for a long, long time anyhow. And so there really wasn't any choice.

With excitement beginning to pound inside him, Barney put out the light, hesitated for just a minute, then let himself out of the shed and into the stream of wind that swirled round the barns. The shock of it took his breath, and the wet soft snow flayed against his face. But he steadied a little inside as he realized that it wasn't really very cold, that the wind whistled more than it cut.

Crossing the big corral, he stepped through the bars and was out on open range. And now that it was done, a curious new calm came over him – to be going somewhere that he had decided for himself. He looked back in the heavy white haze of the storm, saw that the wind was already beginning to blow his tracks away, and it struck him that maybe the weather was a piece of luck after all. Because if they missed him before morning, they wouldn't know which way to look. They'd never figure that he would plough straight into the wind and head for the most dangerous country in the north-west – the gold camps. All at once Barney felt as if he'd just grown two or three inches.

He tried to pace himself, to keep from walking too fast, because he knew he'd have to keep on going. The minute the snow let up, they'd be coming to roust him out, no matter what time of night it was, since they meant to send him on the chuckwagon and that always moved out ahead of the round-up.

After what seemed like hours and hours of trudging along, head-down against the storm, he started to feel a little thinned out inside and would have liked to rest a while. He'd almost decided to try to find some shelter where he could hold up a minute and get his breath when all at once, as if somebody had slammed a door on it, the wind died and left the snow falling straight down with a steady hushed sound. Then at once the snow began to slacken off too, and so Barney slogged ahead as fast as he could. His tracks now showed plainly, without the wind to wash them away. He kept looking behind him and worrying about it until he began to catch up with some other tracks – so new they hadn't filled with snow yet, heavy wheel ruts in the soft wet ground. He set himself to walk in them, and it wasn't long before he heard voices ahead, topped a rise and saw lanterns.

There were three wagons drawn up beside the river, odd-looking old boxes, high and square-topped. At first Barney thought they were hearses, and then he realized they were too big for that. He hesitated, keeping back out of the range of the lights, watching the three men fret up and down the river-bank. The Beaverhead was running high from the May thaw, and this was no place to cross with wagons.

He had a notion to go down to them – it was plain that these were strangers to the Valley and wouldn't recognize him. But he was thinking, you never could tell about older folks or how they'd look at a kid being out alone at night. On the other hand, now that it had stopped snowing, there was no time to waste, and getting across the river was one of the things he hadn't been able to figure out ahead of time. It came to him that this might be a good chance to reach the other side without getting wet. He decided to take the risk.

As he came up, one of the men, a short dumpy little fellow, was talking in a flat way of speech that reminded Barney of back east.

'I say we missed the road and gone clean to Alasky!'

The other, a tall man, answered in a voice thin and crackling and precise as a schoolteacher's. 'This is no time for levity, Hoke.'

'I ain't jokin',' insisted the first. 'Doc, there can't be no place in the Yew-nited States where it snows in June.'

'We are not in the United States,' said the tall man. 'We are in the Territory of Montana, which, they say, is subject neither to the laws of man nor nature. You're quite right about our having missed the road, however, and I don't like the looks of that water.'

'I say we better camp right here.'

'And face the possibility of the river being even higher tomorrow? No, I think not.' From the positive way he spoke, Barney thought the tall man must be in charge. 'We may not have strayed too far from the beaten path. Billy, take a lantern and go upstream.'

'Yes, suh.' The third one of the group turned to obey, and the light glinted off his dark skin. He was a coloured boy, not much older than Barney.

In fact, there wasn't anything dangerous-looking about any of them. Barney threw off his hesitation and walked forward.

'Excuse me,' he said.

All three started, and the one called Hoke raised his lantern so that the yellow light fell in a wider circle. Barney was glad the Mackinaw and cap covered him up so they couldn't notice that he was all knees and elbows and wing-bones.

Even so, the thin man said, 'Why, it's just a child!'

Barney tried to stand a little taller. 'I happened to be passing by and saw you were in trouble, so I thought maybe I could give you a hand.'

The fat little man began to chuckle, but the other one made a small movement of his finger and the chuckle stopped.

'That's kind of you, young man,' the tall one said gravely. 'Do you live hereabouts?'

'No,' Barney spoke up briskly. 'I'm just passing through. Been visiting relatives up the Valley, but I'm on my way north now, to join my father.' It sounded fairly good to him, because he could say it with some truth. For a moment he was almighty glad his mother had spent that time teaching him how to act. He thought, if this gentleman was really a doctor, he'd appreciate good manners. The man was looking at him in such a way that Barney found it hard to keep his eyes steady. The tall man had an odd face, long and narrow, the skin very white and soft. His cheeks were drawn in, and the nose was thin; the mouth was just a straight, pale line, and the eyes were pale, too, in the lantern light – their black centre spots were just points, sharp as needles.

'We'd be grateful for your assistance, my boy,' he said without a hint of a smile. 'What did you have in mind?'

'Well, it's just that you've missed the stage road – you've been following the old trail. But right below here the stream widens – it spreads out shallow and the bottom is mostly gravel. You could probably take these wagons across without getting stuck. I'll show you, if you'd like me to.'

'Good lad!' The tall man pulled a piece of silver out of his pocket.

Barney thought he could have used it, but he shook his head. 'All I want is to ride along on your wagon when you cross, if you don't mind.'

'A modest request!' The doctor bowed a little. 'Delighted to have you.'

So Doc and Barney climbed on to the box of one wagon while Hoke took charge of one of the others and the coloured boy went to drive the third. For all that he seemed up in years, Doc moved lightly and knew how to handle a team. It seemed odd to watch him work the lines with beautiful long soft white fingers that were heavy with rich-looking rings, flashing in the lantern light. Barney was taking stock of the rest of his clothing, the high beaver hat, a heavy black fur coat that reached below his knees, and shoes of the thinnest sort of leather. It wasn't exactly the dress for a teamster, and neither was the man's talk.

As they drove along the river-bank, he was asking questions

17

about the weather and the country. Barney, who hadn't ever been spoken to this way, like an equal, answered up as if he'd lived here all his life. Yes, he said, you could certainly expect a snow in June in these parts. And no, it wouldn't last long; the chinook would start to blow tomorrow, most likely. And then he had to explain that a chinook was a warm south-west wind that would eat the snow up like a cat licking up spilled cream. The man listened to all this and nodded.

'And where are you heading, sir?' the doctor inquired politely.

'Virginia City,' Barney answered with hardly any hesitation.

'Indeed? What a coincidence! That happens to be our own destination. How far would you say we are from it?'

'I'm not sure,' Barney admitted. 'I've never been there. But I've heard it's about two days on horseback, so I suppose with the wagons you might make it in three, unless you get stuck somewhere.'

This didn't seem to please Doc. He frowned and pinched his lips together tight. 'We'd hoped to reach there tomorrow. Our horses need rest and food, and we've run out of grain. It didn't occur to us to provide ourselves with fodder for them, thinking, as we did, that there would be good pasture along the way. We certainly had not suspected that winter would not yet have departed.'

'There's plenty of pasture,' Barney said, puzzled. 'There's grass all over the place underneath the snow.'

'Dead grass is hardly enough sustenance for teams pulling a heavy load, I fear.'

'My uncle fattens his cattle on it,' Barney insisted. 'He leaves the herd out all winter and markets the beeves in the spring. This is bunch grass up here – it's not like ordinary grass, it's rich food, dry or green. Your horses will do fine on it.'

In the light of the swinging lantern, the doctor looked at him again. 'A veritable treasure of information,' he murmured, as if he were thinking out loud. Barney felt fairly pleased, but a little odd, too, because he got the idea there were some things in the tail man's mind that he wasn't saying.

At the bend of the stream they put the wagons across safely enough, the swirling dark water never rising above the hubs. On the other side they pulled up together and Hoke called out, 'Well, Doc, what's it to be? Shall we go on or make camp?'

'We'll stop here.' The doctor was starting to tell about the grass, but Barney, on the listen for any extra noises, had picked up the sound of hoof-beats coming fast from across the river. He began to scramble off the seat of the wagon. When he was almost to the ground Doc reached out and got hold of the collar of the Mackinaw and hauled him like a pup back on to the seat again.

'Why the hasty departure, lad?' he asked with a knowing gleam in his eyes.

Barney squirmed at the delay. 'You hear those horses? It's me they're after. It's my uncle – he's trying to keep me from going to find my father. Please, I've got to hide!'

'And why does your uncle want to keep a boy from his father?'

'He thinks Dad's dead. But I don't. Please. . . .' He tried again to twist loose. 'If they catch me, they're going to send me back to Pittsburgh.'

'Get down,' said the doctor. 'Quickly. There by my feet. No, don't be a fool! There's no time for you to hide anywhere else.'

And Hoke groaned out aloud. 'You crazy, Doc?'

'Be quiet.' The words snapped like a whip.

Barney scrounged down as small as possible on the bottom of the driver's box, and Doc drew part of the fur coat over him.

Just in time, too, for the horsemen were already pounding across the river, heading for the light of the lanterns.

They pulled up short and Barney heard Uncle George's voice. 'What in blazes is this outfit?' He sounded mad.

'This, sir,' said Doc smoothly, 'is a scientific organization devoted to the unselfish benefit of mankind. We are on our way to the communities to the north, to try in our little way to do what good we can. . . .'

'Have you seen a kid tonight as you came along?'

'A child? Merciful heavens, no! Out in this storm?' Doc sounded truly shocked. 'How dreadful! Where did you lose the little tike, sir?'

'We didn't lose him. He's run away. A half-growed boy about so high, skinny little runt, no more meat on him than a ground squirrel.'

'And twice as foolish,' put in one of Uncle George's sons, shouting in a deep voice as if everybody were ten miles away. 'I say he ain't got the starch to walk this far on a clear day, much less head-on into the wind. He musta gone south.'

'If he did, the others'll find him,' said Uncle George shortly. 'I ain't so sure. I could've swore we picked up a track back there a ways.'

'It may have been ours,' said Doc. 'Our boy, Billy, there on the third wagon, often walks ahead in order to search out the way for our wagons, heavily loaded as we are with scientific equipment. . . .'

Barney's uncle cut in impatiently. 'Mebbe. Anyhow, it ain't doin' us no good to stand here and make talk. Come on, he's probably folded up under the snow back there somewheres.' And without a 'thanks' they went splashing back across the ford and off up the bank at a gallop, soon to disappear into the darkness.

Beginning to breathe again, Barney straightened up out of his crouch and unkinked his legs. Hoke was mopping his head with a big white kerchief.

'Jee-hosaphat!' he wheezed as he climbed down off his wagon. 'The chances you take, Doc! We could all get tarred and feathered, helpin' a runaway kid, you know that?'

'One good turn deserves another.' The tall man swung down, too, and held out a hand to help Barney. 'My boy, if you are wondering why I chose to save you from the ultimate horrors of Pittsburgh, just accept the fact that it happens to be a town which, upon occasion, has treated me unkindly and I'm glad to have robbed it of a clever young citizen. Also, I believe every boy needs his father, and I admire your courage in going out to search for him. It strikes me that since we travel in a common direction, we may be of help to each other. I would be glad to furnish you transportation in return for some slight services on your part. In other words, sir, I'm offering you a job.'

Barney had never until now considered taking a job. 'What would I have to do?' he asked.

'Nothing very strenuous. A few chores. For instance, right now you might help Billy unhitch the teams.'

That seemed fair enough and was the kind of work that Barney didn't mind. Much as he believed he could have made it to Virginia City alone, it was too good a chance to turn down – to find someone going his way, not only willing to give him a ride but treating him with a kindness and respect he'd hardly ever known before. And these were people of importance, too. There was an air of grandeur about the tall man – not just his manner and his clothing, but the positive way he'd spoken to Uncle George, rolling the words impressively as if he had marbles in his mouth, and lying so quick and confident.

Barney had never learned the knack of that himself. If he tried to say an outright falsehood, it always stuck in his throat. He thought it must take a great deal of spirit to be able to come out with a whacking good lie while the live evidence was bunched down right between your feet.

As they unhitched the horses, he tried to draw a little talk out of Billy and find out what scientific things these people did, but the coloured boy seemed frightened and would hardly mutter a word. Barney wondered at it a little.

When they got the horses staked out to graze in an open spot where the wind had driven most of the snow off, they came back to find a fire going and a pot of stew warming over it. Barney was surprised to see a woman standing there, stirring with a long-handled spoon. She was plump as a doughnut, hardly any taller than himself, and dressed up like one of the gipsies that sometimes came along the Valley, begging to read fortunes. She wore a spangled yellow skirt and a red shawl round her shoulders. At her feet sat a curly little poodle, black as tar against the snow. It got up idly wagging its tail at Barney, and the woman turned to look at him. Whether it was because the firelight made her eyes look flat as dirty dish-water, or because of the big golden ear-rings casting shadows across her face, Barney was suddenly uneasy. And then she smiled at him in a way that put dimples in her fat little cheeks and he thought he must have been wrong in his judgement.

As everybody took their plates of stew, Doc said, 'I believe that introductions are in order. What may we call you, lad?'

Barney told them his name, and Doc made a slight bow. 'As for us: I am Dr Primus D. Cathcart, this is my associate, Professor Charles Withrow, better known as Hoke, and this, his charming wife, Maddie, a lady of many abilities – not the least of which is her talent as a cook.'

It was pleasant enough, Barney thought, and the stew spread a comfort in his belly, easing the tightness of his nerves and letting the full burden of weariness come down on him in a pile. He could hardly keep his eyes open.

Heavy-headed, he went about helping Billy clean up, only distantly aware that the others had drawn apart and were speaking low, although the snatches of talk that came through to him made him struggle, sleepily, to listen.

'... prove useful in many ways,' Doc was saying quietly, 'and will certainly solve one of our problems, at least temporarily.'

'You mean you'd risk putting that kid into *that* wagon?' Hoke sounded disapproving, and Barney thought it was himself they were talking about.

The mutter went on a while and then Maddie spoke out in a small womanish voice. 'Nonsense! I say nothing like that's going to happen again. Hoke, you got to face it, that little fool Billy has got a chicken gizzard – you ain't going to get him in that wagon again at the point of a scattergun. I'm tired of you doin' all his chores for him. Of course we can use a new boy!'

Billy heard her, too, and looked at Barney for one frightened instant as they put the fire out together. Then the coloured boy turned and went straight to the wagons, climbed up on the seat of one and pulled a blanket over him, leaving Barney to go over to where the others still stood. They fell silent as he came up.

'I was just wondering where I should sleep,' he said.

'Ah, yes, my lad.' Doc nodded. 'I suppose for tonight you'd better stay in my wagon – there's an extra pallet there, you'll see it in the corner. Here's the lantern. I'll be joining you soon to seek some slumber myself.'

Barney took the light drowsily. Giving a yawn that nearly stretched his jaws out of joint, he stumbled over to one of the wagons, went round to the door at the back and had his hand on it when Doc's voice stopped him short.

'Not that one!'

And, looking up, he saw that it was secured by a big shiny new padlock.

So he went on to the next, where he found the door open. Inside, he picked his way through the clutter of trunks and cardboard boxes, bundles of papers and rolls of coloured silk. There was a bunk attached to the wall of the wagon, and over in the corner he found a narrow cotton mattress on the floor. It was a hard bed, but he was past caring just then. Without even taking his shoes off, he flopped down and pulled a blanket over him, as Billy had done. And yet, tired as he was, there was enough curiosity left in him to wonder what it was they had locked up inside the other wagon.

2

In the bright crystal morning light of that next day after the snow, things looked different. The wagons turned out to be a handsome red with gilt lettering on the sides:

Dr Cathcart's Scientific
Research Organization

*Dedicated to the Propagation of Good Health
and the Easing and Prolonging of Life*

It was all done up with the finest curlicues. On top of the lead wagon was a large square object covered with a tarpaulin, probably some of the heavy scientific equipment that Doc had mentioned.

The tall man was as impressive by daylight as at night. Although he still wore the fur coat, he had taken off the beaver hat, and his grey hair gleamed like silk in the sun. Barney, sitting beside him on the box again, felt proud to ride with such a group as this, and his spirits rose high as the team lumbered north along the river-bank. Glancing back, he saw Hoke and Maddie driving just behind, Billy bringing up the rear with the third team.

That locked door still made Barney wonder. They had taken a pail of water and some food into that wagon this morning, then come out and fastened it again. He couldn't help being curious – and then he roused, with a start, to realize that Doc was speaking to him.

'You say you believe we'll cross the stage-coach road some-where below here?'

'Yes, sir.' Barney hoped so, at least. He hoped they'd start moving a little faster. 'I think we'll pick it up pretty soon.' But as he looked around at the mountains, everything seemed out of proportion. The Tendoys seemed far behind in the south-west, and here were the Rubies, glistening under their coat of new snow, big and close above him, while ahead he could see, clearer than ever, the high icy crags of the Tobacco Roots – which meant Alder Gulch. It gave him a strange tight feeling to remember some of the tales he'd heard about the Gulch and about Virginia City.

All that morning the doctor kept asking questions – peculiar questions, though Barney was careful not to let on that he thought they were odd and tried to answer straight and polite. The doctor's mind seemed to skip from one thing to another – the mountains, the gold, especially people and their health.

'Do the good folk of this region suffer any particular ill-nesses?' he asked. 'When the flowers are out, do you notice that many people have colds, coughs, sniffling, and stopped heads?'

Barney didn't think so. 'Some of the cattle get hold of loco-weed and go crazy, though,' he said.

'Interesting indeed. And how about the local superstitions?' Doc persisted. 'Any folk-stories about the weather? Or plant-ing? Ranching?'

Barney remembered a rumour about a herd of wild horses – supposed to be all black and fierce, horses that could never be caught. They said the leader was a stallion that came down out of the hills at night and tempted the ranch mares away to join his outlaw herd. He couldn't see why the doctor should show such interest in a story like that.

'But in this inclement country aren't there cases of recurring rheumatisms? Chilblains? Neuralgias?' Doc asked impatiently. 'What are the special health hazards of panning gold?'

All Barney could think of was the unhealthy aspects of getting bush-whacked for your money. 'I guess since the Vigilantes cleaned up the Gulch,' he said soberly, 'people don't get killed right out on the streets any more, but they say a man can turn up in a back alley with a hole in his head almost any night. I guess that's the worst hazard up there. Virginia is still a rough town.' He was repeating what the old prospector had said – the whiskery old man who had stopped by the ranch on his way back south from the camps not so long ago. After they'd fed him and given him some of Uncle George's pilgrim whisky, he'd got to talking about the Gulch.

'Vigilantes?' Doc was saying. 'And who are the Vigilantes?'

Barney shifted round on the seat uncomfortably. Because when he had asked the same question of the old miner, the man had squinted at him, his black eyes shiny as a couple of jet beads in the firelight. 'That ain't a question to ask, young 'un,' he'd muttered. 'The Vigilantes is this!' And he'd leaned forward to make some marks with a charred ember on the hearthstone: 3–7–77. 'Anybody asks questions about that,' he said, 'is like to have to leave town fast, lyin' low fer black ducks.' Barney hadn't understood it, but he could still remember the funny look on Aunt Norah's face as she rubbed out the numbers with her shoe after the old prospector had gone.

Of course, there had been other men who had talked more freely. Now, with Doc waiting, Barney tried to recollect what he could. 'They say that a while back Virginia City got so wild that the lawful folks either had to leave or get killed or something,' he told the doctor. 'They had a sheriff, but some people noticed that he was always away from town just when the stagecoach got held up, so the honest men joined together and formed

27

their own law. They hunted the outlaws down and caught them. In one month, I heard, they hanged more than thirty men, every one of them a murderer. The sheriff turned out to be the gang leader.'

'You mean to say these gentle citizens dispensed with their own fellow men, just like that?' Doc murmured thoughtfully. 'How firm!'

'Well, they had trials, they had juries. And it cleaned up the town, so it must have been a good thing. And, besides, they disbanded. I heard they just went back to their homes, and nobody ever mentions who they were – so it's better not to ask, that's all.'

But that wasn't all. Barney was thinking of another man, a younger one, who had stopped in at the ranch, also riding south. He'd laughed, kind of sourly. 'Vigilantes gone? Maybe. But then why do the numbers still turn up on somebody's door? So nobody has to git out of town. That place ain't for me. I like to know where my law's comin' from.' Barney decided not to mention that to Doc, though, or he might not want to go there.

He was relieved when Doc said, 'Well, lad, this is an interesting thing to know, but the years heal many wounds. I doubt if we have anything to worry about.'

'Not so long as you're a doctor,' Barney agreed. 'Everybody needs doctors. Are you a real one?' Because he'd heard that there were some men who got called that just because they'd been to school, even though it had nothing to do with setting bones or rolling pills.

The tall man smiled. 'I prefer to think of myself in a higher sense, as a healer. A doctor can only prescribe for bodily ailments. I try to mend both body and mind, and lead the way to the paths of physical harmony.'

'Is Hoke a doctor, too?'

'He is my scientific assistant – a professor of psychology and other learned studies. Together we have brought health and optimism to millions of suffering people. We are all suffering, Barney. Can you truly say that there has ever been a time when there was not an ache in you somewhere, of the head or heart or bone? You may not even have been aware of it – many people go bravely along ignoring their infirmities. We try to educate them to recognize their symptoms. When we reach our destination, you will see how rewarding this work is. In fact, I've been hoping you would like to stay on with us and participate, at least until you catch up with your father. What can you do? Are you an acrobat? Can you work a rope or recite the Declaration of Independence?'

Barney wondered what that had to do with healing sick people.

Doc was happy to explain. 'A little entertainment is the first principle of helping people – it relaxes their internal tensions and frees their minds of crass suspicion. When the audience has had its spirits enlivened by laughter or wonder at the performance of some feat of skill, I find them far more receptive to my help. The bally is an absolute essential to my theory of treatment.'

Barney had noticed that the doctor liked to roll off big clinkers of words that he could only guess at, but the word 'bally' had a different ring to it that he couldn't put a finger on. 'A trade term, my boy,' Doc explained. 'A piece of vernacular that I couldn't really translate. Where was I? Oh, yes, I was asking if you have any talents.'

'No, sir, I reckon not.'

'Too bad.' The doctor sighed. 'We all contribute to the Show in one way or another.'

29

For a while he was so silent and sober that Barney felt ashamed of himself for not being able to 'contribute'. At last he said, 'Well, I did used to sing – a long time ago when my mother was alive.' And the thought of that brought a tight squeeze to his throat because it had been so long since those days when he and Mother and Dad had all been together.

'Do you suppose you still could?' asked Doc doubtfully.

'I don't know. My voice has gone kind of rusty since then.'

'Well –' the doctor smiled kindly – 'I suppose I could teach you the Declaration of Independence. Try repeating after me – we'll see how quickly you learn. "When in the course of human events, it becomes necessary. . . ."'

Barney tried to keep his mind on it, but just then they were passing old Beaverhead Rock, the rugged bluff that marked the far end of the Valley; it was as far north of the ranch as Barney had ever been before. To see that landmark inch away behind them gave him an empty feeling in the pit of his belly. Of course he'd known all along that there couldn't be any going back, but now it seemed more like a nailed-down fact.

With the horses holding up well, they kept travelling steadily the next three days. While they seemed not to move fast, once they were on the stage road the miles kept rolling back away from them. After the road left the Valley and turned up the Ruby River, the silent steep land began to close in on both sides of them, rugged and dangerous, a fit place for men with guns to look for gold.

Then, late one afternoon, they came to where the road took off up one of the little creeks that fed the Ruby, and Barney thought, with a new fierce twinge of excitement, that this must be the beginning of the Gulch!

They had begun to pass houses – or, rather, shacks knocked together out of scrap timbers and tin and tarpaulins. All along the stream bank were piles of gravel heaped beside odd-looking wooden contraptions. Barney supposed these were the 'rockers' his father had told him about in one letter, the sluice boxes for washing gold out of the sand.

As the shanties grew thicker, the road got worse – rutted and slippery with melting snow. The uphill pull began to tire the horses, and it got so bumpy that Maddie had to come out of her wagon and sit on the box with Hoke. Barney couldn't help but wonder about whatever was in the third wagon, but nobody else mentioned it, so he didn't either.

He was trying to swallow his disappointment over the huddled little districts they were passing. He'd always thought of gold camps as having big fancy hotels and handsome mansions for all the people who'd got rich off their panning, but there wasn't a single house, so far, that was even solid-built. Some of the buildings had the word 'Saloon' written in cracked black paint over the swinging doors, and the men who came out to stare at the wagons were bearded and dirty. By the time they'd gone a few miles they had collected quite a crowd, idling along beside the wagons and making catcalls at Maddie or hollering scornful remarks about Doc's tall hat.

It didn't seem to bother the doctor. In fact, he got more cheerful as they went on. 'I had no idea we'd find such a wealth of population,' he remarked once.

Barney didn't think the population looked very wealthy. The hurtful thought kept coming back to him that one of these ragged men might even be his father. But as he searched their faces, he could hardly believe John Morgan would have any truck with these grinning fellows. Their eyes seemed charged with something dangerous, a disrespect for these fine doctors – for the woman. In fact, it seemed to spread out into a mockery against everything. Their shouts had a rude taunting ring.

31

Barney thought it was probably men like these that the Vigilantes had hung, and he almost wished there were some Vigilantes around now.

It was getting dark when they finally reached an open spot of ground that was fairly level. Doc halted the team. Picking out one of the followers who had been the noisiest, he beckoned the man over.

Loud enough for everyone to hear, he said, 'We've come to this spot on an errand of mercy, sir. We bring vital information, all absolutely free, of course, which may save the life of every person who listens to me.'

The man's smirk seemed to come undone a little, for the words were spoken with a terribly solemn ring.

'Now, then,' went on Doc, as the other quietened, 'can you tell me, sir, how far we are from Virginia City?'

'Virginie?' The man picked at the dirty folds of his collar with an uneasy finger. 'Oh, she's about ten mile on up the Gulch, I reckon.'

'In that case, we prefer to remain here. I can see that there are sufferers among you in need of our help.' Doc chucked to the team and the wagons turned off the road and into a big meadow. The melting snow became a hash of wheelmarks and hoofprints as they drove into a semicircle, with Doc's wagon nearest the road, the others arranged on either side at a slight angle, so that the teams could be taken out of harness.

Barney fretted through the unhitching, staked out his share of horses as fast as he could. Then, without asking whether there was more work to be done, he skirted the crowd and headed up the road on foot. It seemed to him there must be other people than these loafers, people who might have known his father.

A hundred yards above the camping-ground he found a

public house where there was a faro table and several poker games were going. As he entered, a big man in a flat-crowned hat got up off a stool near the door and blocked his way.

'Hold on, bub, this house ain't fer babies to play.'

'I'm looking for a man named John Morgan,' Barney told him with as much dignity as he could gather.

'Never heard of him. On yer way, now. . . .'

In the gathering dusk, he walked on up the road, past other swinging doors – saloons, dance halls with bright yellow light streaming from them, where he could see rouged-up girls in glittering dresses dancing with the rough lot of miners. Barney didn't go in to inquire; his father wouldn't go into such places. But he did stop some of the men on the road to ask his question. They answered curtly, told him they knew no Morgan, and one of them cursed him, for no reason, and brushed him out of the way. The tone of hate about these people reminded him of Uncle George – it was as if the bigger they were, the more they scorned the presence of a boy among them. Discouraged, Barney went on, looking for some respectable place where he might get information, but there wasn't any. As darkness folded down over the Gulch, loud talk began to rise from the bar-rooms and hurdy-gurdies – guffaws of laughter and drunken singing.

Feeling more lonely than ever before in his life, Barney hesitated. He came to a halt on the edge of the shadowy roadway with its swaggering traffic. Once he had to jump back quickly as a band of horsemen clattered past unheeding. He knew he ought to go on with his search, but actually all he wanted right then was to get back to the people who had treated him fairly. As night settled in, it was getting cold, and he realized that he'd probably missed supper. But what was worse, he knew, was that he'd skipped off without asking, or finishing his chores.

As Barney began to walk slowly back down the road, he kept hearing a sound in the distance, a strange screeching music that got louder and brighter as he walked. He noticed that other people were going in his direction, hurrying. The music made him want to hurry too – it made a buzz of excitement in him, weird as demons squalling. It kept reminding him of something – and then he knew what it was! The ear-splitting marvellous whistle of a calliope, like the one back at the fair in Pennsylvania. But what would a calliope be doing here? he wondered.

And then, all at once, he knew where it was coming from, and he started to run. Sure enough, the crowd was gathered in the field where the wagons were camped.

The bally had begun.

3

WHEN Barney had worked his way up to the front, he saw that they had pitched a good-sized tent at the back of the wagons, where it would be sheltered from the wind. The flap of the tent was near one end of the platform, while the other end of the platform was right beside the door of Doc's wagon. Strung out over the front of the platform was a banner of blue silk bearing the words:

DR CATHCART'S MIRACLE SHOW

What with the noise of the calliope, Barney missed what Hoke had said, but now Billy appeared on the stage dressed in baggy pink satin trousers and a tight gold shirt, a white turban round his head that made his brown face look twice as dark as usual. He had an armload of Indian clubs, which he set up in a row in front of him, like ninepins. Then, picking them up two at a time, he began to juggle them, adding more and more until he had them all in the air, spinning up end over end and coming down and up again, so fast and easily that Barney thought he'd never seen anybody's hands work with such a smooth skill.

Hoke kept nodding and shouting to the crowd. 'Look at this boy! Look at him go!' Finally Billy caught the clubs and ducked inside the tent. At the same time somebody cut off the calliope so that Hoke's voice sounded hushed and confidential in the sudden stillness as he leaned out from the edge of the platform and spoke to the audience.

'He's just gone to get some more props, folks. When he gets a good audience like you, he wants to put on some real tough tricks. He can juggle anything – wineglasses, dinner plates, knives, and tommyhawks. Now, I don't want you to think we're here to take any money for this show. No, sir, we just want you to have a little fun. We count it our blessing to spread pleasure around the world, and we take our reward from that – yes, sir. We just want . . .'

At that moment the curly black poodle walked across the platform behind him, balancing on its stiff little back legs, hugging a pink parasol in its front paws, about as silly a thing as Barney had ever seen. He had to laugh and so did everybody else in front, which made the people at the back press closer to see.

'Well, now, if that ain't a dog fer you!' Hoke pretended to be disgusted. 'Give her a trick to do in the show and she'll *hound* you to death with it.'

The audience thought this was pretty funny. They haw-hawed and poked each other in the ribs.

Hoke nodded. 'That's all we want to do – make you laugh, make you wonder a little. You all know there's more powerful forces than most normal human bein's know about, things like mental telepathy and thought transference. But did you know *you* may actually be one of them people with a extry brain dimension? It's your brain raises you higher than the dumb animiles, my friends, and I believe you look like an exceptional bunch of fellows. I'm gonna actually find out if there ain't some strong thinkers among you. I'm gonna prove you can transfer your thoughts to somebody else without you speakin' a blessed word. Of course, it takes a real gifted person to pick up these thoughts, as that's a good deal harder to do, so I'm gonna introduce you to a rare and gracious lady, she's had a high esteem in Europe *and* the Continent. . . .' Hoke was escorting Maddie out on to the platform. 'Yes, sir, this little lady is one of the greatest mind-readers in the world, folks. Madame Medea!'

She had put on a long piece of black lace over her gipsy dress and wore a little glittery cap on her frizzy grey hair. As she sat down, Hoke drew out a piece of black cloth.

'Now, just to prove to you that these is real powers of thought and there ain't no chance of it bein' a trick, I'm gonna blindfold the lady so's you'll be certain-sure that she can't see what I'm doin' or what you're doin'. . . .' He tied the cloth in place over her eyes. 'Now, then, I'm comin' down and walk among you.' He stepped down into the midst of the miners. 'You, sir – ' he picked out a man – 'I want you to choose some article of your personal property, hold it in your hand – no, I don't want to touch it. I just want you to concentrate on it. Now bear down hard!'

Barney edged over close enough to see that the man had a big gold watch in his hand.

'Madame Medea?' called Hoke. 'You pickin' up any thoughts?'

'Many – many – thoughts.' She spoke in a mysterious hollow voice, swaying back and forth a little. 'Someone out there is thinking of his woman-friend. Her name is "Lizzie".'

'Now, that ain't what we want!' protested Hoke, while two of the miners joshed a third one, who turned very red in the face. 'Some of you all have pretty powerful thoughts,' Hoke said, grinning. 'All right, now, you fellow, concentrate again, concentrate good.'

The man with the watch frowned and the crowd grew still.

'It – is – a – watch,' Maddie chanted, in a voice that made every man-jack of the crowd shiver.

'You're right, and a mighty beautiful one it is,' agreed Hoke. While the men murmured over this, he went on. 'It's got three engraved initials on the back. What a fine article! I wonder if you'd just concentrate on them, sir, and she'll tell you what they are. You got a powerful brain there, friend. She's gettin' you good.'

The miner's face set hard. In the silence Maddie began to sway again. All at once she said, 'The initials are W-F-A.'

The man stared around at his neighbours. 'Hit it right on the head!'

And now everybody wanted to try. Hoke walked among them a while, and every answer Maddie called out was a hundred per cent correct. Barney had a chilly feeling inside that she might be reading his own mind any minute. Finally, though, she announced she was tired, and Hoke, promising the audience she'd be back, led her off the stage. Even before she was out of sight, here came the foolish little dog again, with the pink parasol.

While they were chuckling at that, Hoke began to hand out bunches of leaflets, saying, 'Take one and pass 'em on, please. Absolutely free. Take one and pass 'em on, that's it.'

Barney got hold of one as they came past him, and in the light of the flares made out that it was a copy of a newspaper article with a picture of Doc. The headline read: CATHCART DISCOVERS THE SECRET OF RENEWED VIGOUR!

Hoke was saying, 'Of course, this is the part of the programme you've really been waiting for. You've all heard of that eminent scientist Dr Primus D. Cathcart, world-renowned researcher on human diseases, author of that famous book *You*

Don't Need to Die. This clipping you got tells how Dr Cathcart's been in Europe recently so's all them fancy specialists could consult with him. They all want to learn his formulee for restoring a man to be as strong as if he was seventeen, that prime time of your life. I wish I could tell you all about the doctor's discoveries, but I can't. I'm just a poor college man myself, with only an L-L-D and a P-H-D and he's way beyond me. So I'm gonna let him explain it to you in person. Doctor Cathcart, please, sir. . . .'

Doc stepped out of the door of his wagon and on to the platform. Over his handsome clothes he was now wearing a long velvet cape. After Hoke's loud chant, his voice seemed soft and refined.

'As Professor Withrow has told you, my friends, I have been privileged to dedicate my life to the saving of yours – it is for this reason that I've come among you. I want to save any sufferer whose life is ebbing away due to his own carelessness. I want to cure you while you're still on your feet, while the terrible degeneration that's gripping your vital organs is still in its early stages. It may seem to you only a headache or an uneasy stomach. To me it is the sign of deadly disease. You may be wondering what I profit from this work, but I beg of you to think what humble satisfaction one receives in the healing of the sick. Oh, this is by far the greatest payment! My friends, I could have been rich, thanks to the gratitude of all the people I've helped, but I refuse to accept any remuneration for my services. Tonight you've all seen a free show, and now I'm willing to give you, absolutely free, some advice about your health that would cost you many hundreds of dollars at an expensive sanatorium. But the truth is hard to face, my friends. The sad fact is that the perfect age, according to scientific records, is the age of seventeen years, two months and twenty-five days, exactly. If you haven't reached that point, you're on the way up. If you've passed it, you've already started down towards the grave.'

That comforted Barney somewhat, because he had some time to go yet, but Doc's next words took away the satisfaction.

'Moreover, before you can even enjoy this youth while you have it, you must be sure the mechanisms of your body are in perfect working order. Now, maybe you think you're in fairly good health. Well, possibly you are. Or do you sometimes begin to feel tired? Do you dream at night? And when you waken, does it take an effort to drag yourself out of bed? Lack of energy can mean serious deficiencies are tearing at the vitals. In the closing hours of the day you may feel a thirst that cannot be quenched with anything but whisky. This is a dangerous symptom.' He shook his finger warningly. 'Liquor will not help you. Nothing can help you, save one medicament – I mention this just in passing – only one, which contains a strong solution of the native drugs discovered by the Choctaw Indians, the most healing drugs ever known to man. I'm referring, of course, to my own Curative.' As he talked, he took a small bottle from his pocket. 'A distillation of miracle potions which is worth more than its weight in gold. The product of years of scientific research.' Carefully he put it away again. 'One swallow is enough to restore a man to perfect health for several weeks. But since only a relatively few people in the world – royalty, for the most part – will ever be so fortunate as to taste it, then the best I can do is to go around, giving freely what advice I can, to help people ward off the fateful day of their doom, at least temporarily. . . . I beg your pardon, sir?' He leaned forward to listen to a man in the first row.

'I said, how much you sellin' that stuff for, Doc?'

'The Curative?' Doc frowned. 'I hadn't planned on selling

any at all. My own supply is dwindling to where I must dole it out to the afflicted one swallow at a time.' He seemed to hesitate, then sighed deeply, got out the bottle and uncorked it. 'However, when people listen to me sympathetically and with intelligence, I find myself carried away by the need to help them. Here, friend, please accept a taste, absolutely free and at my own expense. It can't hurt you, and no matter what debility has a clutch on you, the magic blend will take hold and clear it up.'

The man put the bottle to his lips and drank, choked a little. 'Well, I'll be boonswoggled.' He looked at the crowd pressing round him and nodded. 'It's sure enough strong.'

Another man called up to Doc. 'Can I buy a swig of that?'

The doctor looked at them helplessly. 'I simply cannot restrain my generosity when sufferers appeal to me. Professor, will you see if there are a few bottles left?'

Hoke went into the wagon. In a minute he came back with half a dozen of the small bottles. 'The full price?' he asked, as with exaggerated care he handed them over.

Doc shook his head. 'To these people I'll let them go at cost – five dollars, no more.'

There was some mumbling about that, but the man who had asked for one stepped up doggedly and put down five silver eagles, and pretty soon Hoke had sold out, while Doc was going on talking.

'Now, my real purpose in coming here was not to sell you medicine, as I told you before. I want to help you all live longer. These fortunate gentlemen availing themselves of the Curative are already well on the way, but the rest of you can profit from certain healthful precepts of living which I intend to impart. Before we go any further, though, I want to show you the living proof of what physical perfection can be achieved – the perfect specimen of a man, whom I have raised from childhood according to the principles which I am divulging to you tonight. Gentlemen, I'm inviting you to come into the tent – absolutely free, of course – and see the strongest man in the world!'

With a grand gesture of his hand, he waved towards the door of the tent, where Hoke stood holding back the flap. He started up a curious sing-song chant. 'Step right in. See him lift one thousand pounds. Samson, the strongest man in the world!'

They crowded inside and Barney with them. The walls of the tent were hung with charts of people's innards. To one side was another low platform flanked by two blazing torches, and at the back, in the shadows, a curtained box with someone sitting in it. At the front of the platform lay a curious thing like the axle of a wagon – a long iron bar with a huge round ball of iron fixed to either end. On each of these weights, painted in white, was the figure 500, large enough for all to see.

When everybody was inside, Doc followed in, too, and Hoke let the tent flap drop behind them, staying outside himself. In the distance Barney heard the calliope start up again, but it sounded far away and didn't interfere with what Doc was saying.

'Now, then, my friends, I must explain that this is no ordinary bar-bell. We had it specially cast out of solid iron – there simply wasn't a weight large enough to establish a new world record for strength. Each end of this bar tipped the scales at over five hundred pounds. But I don't ask you to take my word for it. I invite the strongest one among you to step up here and try to lift just one end of it.'

After some backing and stalling, they pushed forward a husky fellow in faded overalls. He walked up with some embarrassment, bent down and tried to get a grip on one of the ends, but all he could do was roll it round the platform. He straightened up at last, grinning, a little red-faced.

'She's too heavy for me,' he said as he stepped back down.

'Don't be embarrassed, my friend.' Doc smiled at him kindly. 'This bar-bell is too heavy for every man in the world – but one!' He snapped his fingers, and the figure seated in the shadows stood up.

A gasp went through the watchers. In the flickering light of the torches, it didn't look like any ordinary human who stood before them – it was a savage giant of a figure. Long shaggy black hair fell clear to his shoulders, and the lower part of his face was covered with a curly black beard. He was stripped, except for a spotted animal skin which he wore fastened over one shoulder, and Barney had never seen such hard powerful-looking muscle on any man, though he'd always counted Uncle George and the boys as fairly strong. Samson's skin was glistening, sleek as oil, as he moved forward, the light rippled along his body. Then he stood still, the big bone-crushing hands hanging loosely at his sides, his head thrown back with a fierce sort of scorn, as if he didn't want to notice the crowd.

'Can you imagine,' Doc was saying, 'can you picture yourself partaking of the potential energies which you see embodied here? Can you imagine restoring yourself to such a state of vigour? Nature has done this, my friends – the most powerful force in the universe – nature! Nature captures the sun's energies naturally, but I have found the secret to store this vital essence pouring down upon us from the skies, to release it into your own blood stream, so that it can perform the alchemy that will make you as nearly as possible a perfect physical specimen like this.' He was turning the strong man slowly so that they could see all sides of his body. 'Please notice – there is not a trace of flab, no ounce of unnecessary weight, no slightest grotesque muscular development to indicate that his strength is some sort of freakish trick of fate. And yet you will witness what he is capable of.' He stepped back, leaving Samson standing alone in front of the bar-bell.

The strong man reached down, took a good grip with both hands at about the centre of the bar, and with a jerk lifted it to rest against his thighs, just above his half-bent knees, leaning back against the weight. With another swift move he lifted it to shoulder height, arching his body to take the weight on his chest. Then, with a sudden step forward, he thrust it high overhead. For a full moment he stood there, holding it, while the light flickered over the knotted muscles of his arms and shoulders and torso. The audience was breathless.

At last, quickly he lowered it to the ground and stepped a little aside, folded his arms across his chest and stood motionless while Doc went on talking – talking about what the compounds of nature could accomplish if melted down into a pure form. He had another bottle in his hand, a beautiful bottle this time, with a gold seal on the front and a dark liquid inside. He was going to let this Elixir go, he said, for the merest fraction of its worth – just enough to cover the cost of bottling it, because if he were to charge them for his research time and for the hazards of getting the ingredients, which came from the jungles of Ethiopia and Abyssinia, they just plain couldn't afford it. It turned out that this bottle cost only a dollar, and a number of men began to dig down into their pockets, but Barney had almost stopped listening by then.

He was watching Samson, who still stood without moving, although a moth, attracted by the torches, had flown in and was flittering round his head. No matter how near to the strong man's face it wheeled and circled, he never winked or moved a muscle, just stared straight ahead with a cold disdainful set to his face. It reminded Barney of something – he tried to think what – and then he remembered. One of the ranch dogs, a shaggy mean animal, used to sit like that without moving while a fly flirted round his nose. The old dog had never blinked or ducked either, because he was blind.

4

WHEN the last Show was over and the torches had been put out, the crowd dispersed and wandered off. Barney made his way over to stand just outside Doc's wagon, watching the crack of light under the door. He had been doing some sober thinking as the evening wore on.

One thing he knew now – that the Declaration of Independence wasn't ever going to put him up on that stage with Billy and the juggling act. It didn't even stack up very well against the poodle dog's tricks. As far as the chores were concerned, there were plenty of people who could do them – people who didn't fly off without leave at the drop of a hat. He had to admit that Doc would have every right to be mad at him, even fire him from his job. So he shivered there for a minute longer, then steadied his nerve as well as he could and walked up to knock on the door of the wagon.

When Doc opened it, Barney was relieved to see the tall man break out in a smile of welcome. 'Well, my boy, we were beginning to be afraid you'd left us without saying good-bye – and without taking your coat. Glad you dropped back for it.' He reached over and handed the Mackinaw to Barney. 'Oh, and how is your father? Did you bring him along with you?'

Barney shook his head, holding the coat in his hands foolishly without putting it on. 'He isn't here – at least, nobody I talked to had heard of him.'

Doc nodded and frowned. 'It takes time to track a man down,

especially in this country, where people come and go and leave no trace of themselves. He may be just a few miles up the Gulch – or he may be in Alaska by now. At any rate, with your ambition and persistence, I have no doubt you'll find him. Good luck on it, lad.' He held out his hand. Barney took it uneasily. It sounded as if the doctor was saying good-bye.

Drawing in a deep breath, he said, 'I'm sorry I went off without telling you. I was hoping maybe you'd let me keep on working for you a while.'

Doc's eyebrow cocked at a curious angle. He sat down at a little desk which was built into one corner of the wagon, motioning Barney to sit opposite him in the other chair. 'But what about your father?'

'I still want to go on looking for him.' Barney hesitated. 'But I guess I'll need a job for a while and . . . Well, I thought . . . You will keep on travelling, won't you?'

The doctor considered this gravely. 'We travel slowly, but before the summer is over, I'd say we will reach every settled community in the Territory. Of course, whether you can control your impatience and suit your pace to ours – this is a question you should think over seriously, Barney. I don't like to sound unreasonable, but I do like to be able to count on the people who work for me. You'll find that this is the way with most jobs.'

Barney fidgeted uncomfortably on his stool. He was thinking more guiltily than ever that here was the one man who had ever been really helpful to him for no good reason, and yet he had let that man down. He was beginning to be very ashamed.

Doc went on gently, 'I'd thought if you were going to stay with us that I could help you with your search. There are many places that I can go where you could not, and people who would hardly pay attention to your questions will be more respectful if the inquiry comes from me.'

True enough! Barney thought silently.

'I even had in mind a very special job for you. It's really a job for an older person, but you have shown yourself to have unusual courage and, I thought, common sense. . . .'

Barney sat up straight and threw back his shoulders. 'I'd be much obliged for the chance to try it,' he said. 'I promise not to skip off again. Are you going to teach me to juggle?'

'Juggle?' Doc smiled a little. 'I hadn't thought of it. Do you want to learn?'

Barney nodded earnestly. Ever since he had seen Billy working the clubs, he had been itching to try it himself. 'I'm sure I could do it. I'd practise hard –'

'Good. One can never get too many jugglers. We'll give Hoke a chance at you – he's an excellent teacher. In time you may work up enough skill to join in the bally. But that is not what I had in mind. The job I was talking about has to do with our strong man.'

Everything went dead quiet inside Barney. He began to get a fluttery feeling, like butterflies in his stomach, as Doc went on.

'If you saw the Show tonight, you may have realized that Samson is blind. We need someone to act as his companion and serve his needs, which are simple enough. Do you think you could manage such a task?'

Barney swallowed. 'Do you think he'd like me?' he stammered, wishing he felt braver. 'Big men – usually – don't.'

'Samson,' said the doctor dryly, 'doesn't like anybody. He's had a sad history – blind since he was a child, living in a world that is callous towards infirmity. When I first saw him, he was hardly as old as you, being used almost as a beast of labour on a farm down in Oklahoma. I recognized his physical promise and accepted the responsibility of raising him – his parents were glad to get rid of him. I put him under the training of an Oriental wrestler, who taught him to use his body properly. I've nurtured him upon my own formulas and built him into the strongest man in the world. But his mind has never become balanced to the fate of eternal darkness. In spite of all I've done for him, he is, alas, ungrateful. He has a violent temper – at times he's fierce, at other times cold and morose. There are times when I fear that the poor fellow's sanity is gone, such unreasonable hatred he harbours against all of us around him. I tell you all this so that you can judge that it is not an easy job. But Samson is no bully – he'd not hurt you. In fact, I've thought that perhaps the presence of some young person might help quiet his rebelliousness and even soften his harsh moods. Are you game to try it?'

Barney drew a deep breath. 'Do you always keep the door of his wagon locked?'

'Oh, that. . . . No indeed. Only when we're travelling, and then it's for his own protection. When he gets restless, he has a tendency to ignore his utter helplessness. Recently he took a notion to get out of the wagon and walk. We didn't notice it at first, and he became separated from us. We finally caught up with him, far back, wandering along the road in the wrong direction at the mercy of any opportunist he might meet. We had the lock put on to forestall a recurrence of such an accident. Of course, if you were with him, you wouldn't let such a thing happen. You'd come and tell me, so that we could help him and protect him from himself. It's quite a responsibility. Samson detests being helped. In fact, perhaps I'd better sound him out. If you'll wait here a moment, I'll go and talk to him, see how he takes to the idea.'

Barney wished the doctor hadn't gone off so quickly before he had finished making up his mind. Left alone, he stood up and idled around the narrow limits of the wagon. While his mind registered right enough what he saw, he was mostly thinking about what a risky life it might be, acting as squire to the strongest man on earth. It occurred to him that if he hadn't fit around Uncle George, this was going to be the biggest misfit of all. And there was Doc's sober warning that the Show didn't travel fast . . . (in a cabinet behind Doc's desk, the door of which was ajar, he saw four or five dozen bottles of the Elixir) . . . and, too, he thought, a strong man with a bad temper could do a lot of damage without meaning to . . . (there were also some bottles labelled 'Hartshorn', 'Belladonna', 'Red Pepper', and a huge jug of molasses. . . . But, Barney was thinking, he was pretty fast on his feet himself and should be able to keep out of reach of a blind man . . . (there was a large red box on one of the shelves) . . . and, most of all, there was the certain truth that Doc could ask about his father in places that Barney couldn't even get in. This was the biggest consideration. . . .

The door opened and Doc beckoned. 'Come, lad, the plan is satisfactory to Samson.'

Slowly Barney followed him out into the cold night. The padlock was gone from the strong man's wagon. The doctor knocked, then opened the door. It was dark inside, and Barney realized, with a sense of shock, that it didn't matter to the man in there whether there was light or not. Doc held up the lantern and motioned Barney in ahead of him.

Samson was sitting on the bunk, which, like the one in Doc's wagon, was attached to one wall. He was still dressed for his act, the light glinting off his body, which Barney saw now was actually coated with oil. As they came in, he didn't turn his massive head of black hair or give any sign that he heard the doctor speak.

'Here's Barney Morgan, the young man I told you about. He'll be staying here with you for a while.' Doc waited for some response and, when he got none, looked at Barney and shrugged sadly. Then he went on. 'I'm going to leave you two to get acquainted while I go and collect some suitable bedding for the boy.' And, setting down the lantern, he went back outside and shut the door.

Barney glanced round the room. It was a clean neat little chamber – just a bunk and a stand with a wash-basin. A small stove in one corner was giving off a comfortable warmth, but it was not heat that had brought out the sweat under Barney's clothes. There was something about the stillness of the powerful figure on the bunk, hunched over with his elbows on his knees and the big hands hanging loose and ready, that made Barney feel as if the room might explode at any minute.

And yet, when he spoke, Samson's voice was quiet. 'Don't be afraid of me,' he said, with the same scorn that was part of his expression.

'I'm not,' said Barney, as positively as he could.

'Yes, you are. I can smell fear a mile off. You're standing there shaking like a wet chicken. Move around and work it off. Go and put some water on the stove to heat.'

Barney did as he was told, fumbling considerably and wishing that he'd stop smelling like a wet chicken. When he had finished, he turned to face the strong man. 'What else shall I do?'

'Open the window. That lantern's smoking the place up.'

He found a small window in the front panel of the wagon, tilted it open and propped it with a stick. Then he came back to stand – not too near – in front of the strong man.

'Well, what do you look like?' demanded Samson abruptly.

'Not much,' blurted Barney honestly. 'I mean, I'm kind of small and skinny. I wish I had some muscle like you.'

The face didn't change its hardness. 'Oh, you do, eh?'

'Yes, sir. Everybody says I'm a runt.'

'Stop eating worms,' ordered the strong man, 'and don't "sir" me – my name's Steve. Come over here.'

Fighting down an impulse to bolt for the door, Barney determined silently he'd not be thought a coward, smell or no smell, and made himself walk forward. When he was close enough to touch, the man reached out and took hold of him by the shoulders, feeling his ribs and back gently, though Barney could sense the strength lying ready in that grip. He ran his hands down over the boy's waist and took the measurement of his hips.

Feeling awkward and embarrassed, Barney said, 'See what I mean? Pretty puny.' And he tried to laugh it off, but the laugh didn't work right and just sounded like a silly scared giggle.

'Of course you're thin,' growled the man impatiently. 'You're growing. But you're built straight and sound. Besides, it's what's up here that counts –' he thumped a knuckle against Barney's forehead – 'and what's here –' he poked a finger into Barney's middle – 'which remains to be seen. Is that water warm enough to wash in yet?'

Edging out from under his hands, Barney went to see, told him that it was. The strong man shook back the long black hair and clubbed it into a knot at the base of his neck, tying it with a leather strip. Then he bent over the basin and began to wash himself. While he was bathing, Doc came back with an armload of quilts and ticking, which he dumped on the floor in a heap. He gave Barney a look that meant *Is everything all right?* and the boy nodded without much enthusiasm.

'Well, I'll bid you both good night.' The doctor said it pleasantly enough, but Samson didn't answer.

Left alone again with the strong man, Barney felt uneasy in the silence that came over the room. He'd always liked to get away by himself, so he could be still and even listen to the stillness, but when other people were around he expected them to talk. Uncle George and that whole family never stopped talking – loud, too. Now, to have the big man stay silent for so long seemed unnatural to him, and he thought of what the doctor had hinted at – about Samson not being quite right in the head.

At last, out of sheer discomfort, Barney spoke up carefully, trying to choose the right thing to say. 'Do you reckon if I work hard the doctor would give me some of that Elixir so I could put on some weight and get a little stronger?'

Samson made a short disgusted sound. Barney thought for some reason this hadn't been the right question to ask.

'If you're so full of your own littleness,' said the strong man, 'why did you run away from home? Home's where *little* boys belong.' He finished drying himself and tossed the towel at the rack over the basin. It caught and hung there, the aim so sure that Barney began to wonder if the man maybe did have some sight after all. His eyes looked just like anybody's – a light hard blue. He turned to face Barney now, and for a second the boy was almost sure the strong man was really looking at him. He shifted a little to one side to test it, but Samson's look didn't move with him.

'Well, why?' demanded the strong man again, as if he were accusing Barney of something. He spoke with such a rough straightness that there was only one way to answer.

Without thinking, Barney said, just as bluntly, 'I left that house because it was no home of mine! I'm going looking for my father – he doesn't make fun of people who are small!' Then, shocked at his own rashness, he swallowed hard and held his breath, waiting for something violent to happen.

But Samson just turned away, went over to the stove and set about banking the fire. Again the sureness with which he moved, almost as if his fingers had eyes in them, filled Barney with wonder, until the strong man reached for the damper and got hold of the hot stovepipe instead. For a minute he cussed in short blistering words that even Uncle George would have admired.

Abruptly he turned to Barney. 'What are you gawping at? What does all that dead quiet mean? What are you thinking?'

Just as before, his outspoken question startled the truth out of Barney before he had time to take caution over what he said. 'I was just thinking it must be mortal hard to be blind.'

The strong man took a step, reached out and caught hold of him so fast he didn't have time to duck. He got a grip on the back of Barney's neck where a cat picks up her kittens. It didn't hurt, but it could have, any minute.

'Does it seem terrible to you not to have four hands?' he demanded harshly.

'N-no,' stammered the boy.

'But if everybody else had four hands and you didn't, you might start feeling cheated. Especially if they came around and put up a sad mouth about how poor off you were. You'd start feeling sorry for yourself. Right?'

'I g-guess so.'

'And you'd be wasting your time, too. You can build muscle and you can train your mind, but you can't grow an extra set of hands. If you ever start pitying me,' said the strong man with a sort of soft violence, 'you'll go out of here faster than you came in.'

'Yes, sir,' quavered Barney.

The powerful fingers tightened on his neck – enough to make him wince. 'What did I tell you about "sir"?'

'I mean – all right, Steve.'

5

THE next day started off bright enough, with no hint of how bad it was going to turn out. The sun was blazing full and hot, taking off the last of the snow, bringing up a real June smell of sap and green leaves and warming earth. As Barney went about sweeping the wagon and straightening the bunk, he was thinking it was a shame that the strong man couldn't see what a fine day it was.

Samson got surlier by the minute, as if he sensed this pity that he hated. He went about doing his exercises with a scowl, and when Barney paused in his chores to watch and marvel at the strong man's tireless ease, it made Samson even madder.

'Well, what's to stare at?' he growled in small spurts between doing push-ups. 'Didn't you ever – see callisthenics before? Or did you think – the Elixir is – what keeps me in trim? Did you suppose – a man gets strong – without working for it? Get out of here – I don't like to be watched.'

Barney was glad enough to go. He took the breakfast dishes round to where Maddie was washing up, at the back of the tent. Hoke was there, too, seated on a barrel, tipped back against his wagon, playing with a long black-snake whip. He could make it do tricks the like of which Barney had never seen – it rippled and coiled and uncoiled like something alive, reached out like lightning and popped the heads off the dandelions that had come swarming out in the warm melt after the sow.

As he gave the dishes to Maddie, Barney was bothered again by a notion that her eyes didn't belong with the rest of her dimply face. But then he remembered she could tell exactly what was in his mind if she wanted to, so he concentrated on thinking only the nicest things about her and edged towards Hoke.

'Doc said you'd teach me to juggle sometime,' he mentioned tentatively. He was thinking it would be just as well to start as soon as possible, because he could see he wasn't going to last long with Samson.

Hoke nodded. 'He told me you had a hankerin' to learn, but I better warn you, you're gonna have to practise hard or I ain't gonna teach you. Don't bother me unless you're really dead set on it.'

'I am!' Barney assured him earnestly. 'How should I begin?'

Hoke glanced around, beckoned to Billy who had just finished watering the horses. 'We'll see how your coordination is. Some got it, some ain't. All a matter of coordination. Here, Bill, we're gonna do a little tandem act. Go bring the clubs.'

The coloured boy went to where a trunk stood open beside the far wagon – Maddie had hauled all their luggage out into the sunlight and was hanging the clothes on a line to air. Picking two Indian clubs out of the top of the trunk, Billy came back. Hoke gave each of the boys one and stationed them opposite each other, about ten feet apart.

'The idee,' he went on, 'is to throw it just right so's Billy can catch yours and you can catch his. He knows how an' you don't, so you match your throw to his. Just keep thinkin' "catch-and-throw, catch-and-throw". Let's go.'

The first few times, Barney managed to catch Billy's pitch and even though his own throws were wild, the coloured boy got hold of them by being quick. But then Barney got to concentrating so hard on the catch that he threw way over Billy's head and missed the catch anyhow.

'You ain't coordinatin' hard enough,' called Hoke. And as the coloured boy started to go after the clubs, he added, 'Let Barney collect 'em.'

Which was fair enough, of course, since it was his fault they both got away. As he bent down to pick one of them up, something stung him sharply across the tight part of his pants. Barney jumped and straightened in time to see the bullwhip go licking back home to lie at Hoke's feet. He felt himself go red in the face.

Hoke grinned in his usual friendly way. 'Part of my teachin' method. To learn a thing you got to have incentive, and I don't know of no incentive like not wantin' to get snapped on the rump. Go ahead, boy, pick up the other club.'

Barney went over and did as he was told, tried to be quick about it, but he couldn't escape the end of that whip. When he came back with the second Indian club, there were two hot spots on his rear end.

'Now watch what you're doin' a leetle closer,' Hoke said kindly.

So Barney tried harder than ever, but the incentive didn't seem to work for him. The more he got to thinking about the whip, the more fumble-fingered he got, until he couldn't have caught an Indian club in a basket and his own throws were all over the lot.

Finally one went sailing off into one of the open trunks beside Hoke's wagon; it was a big trunk, almost empty just then, and the club was far down on the bottom. It was all Barney could do to bring himself to sprawl over the edge and reach for it. The whip nipped him, of course – in such a tender spot that in jerking away from the pain of it he almost fell into the trunk. As he scrambled around, disarranging the few things left there, he saw part of a poster that was on the very bottom:

WANTED

For Fraud and Extortion

'HOKUM' CHARLIE WILSON
and
'MAD MOLLY' WILSON

Barney got out of the trunk fast, but the puzzle of it stood out in his mind as big and black as the letters of the notice, even though there was no time to figure it out then.

Doggedly he went back to stand in front of Hoke. 'Do you suppose I just don't have any co –?'

'Oh, your coordination will do. We'll make a dandy juggler out of you. Go back now and try it again.'

When Barney took Samson's lunch to him, the strong man seemed amused about something, although it wasn't the kind of humour that lightened the bitterness of his face.

'How does it feel to be a juggler?' he said sardonically. 'And I'll bet you *asked* him to teach you. Begged yourself into a sore backside.' He took his plate of food and began to eat.

'If that's what it takes to learn, then I'll get sore until I learn,' Barney said stiffly, feeling fairly noble.

'Go ahead. Juggling's useful to know. Juggling makes the world go round.' The strong man let out a mirthless laugh. 'And especially don't ever question Hoke; if he says a welt across the rump will make your hands work better, by all means believe him.'

Barney had to think about that one. He was still pondering it when, as he was taking the dishes to be washed, Doc called him over and said he had another task for him – he and Billy were to go up into the hills and collect some wood to fire the calliope.

He was glad for an excuse to get away from camp for a little while – there were plenty of things to be figured out. He wished the coloured boy wasn't so shy, and as they climbed the long slope behind the Gulch he studied Billy curiously, wondered how old he really was. The lean bony frame was a little more muscular than his own, and the sorrowful brown face seemed somehow wiser. He wished he could ask a few questions.

It was a lazy afternoon with the sun hot on their backs and a quiet stir of air coming down off the high parts of the mountains. Tentatively Barney said, 'I don't seem to catch on to Indian clubs very fast. Do you think I'll ever be a juggler?'

The coloured boy glanced at him fearfully, and when he spoke, his voice was gaspy and soft with shyness.

'What-for you want to learn jugglin'?'

'So I can stay with the Show,' Barney told him. 'Like Doc said, everybody's got to contribute.'

The little Negro shook his head, speaking almost in a whisper. 'What-for you want to go 'long with these folks? You don't got to. You could light on off whilst you don't yet belong. Mist' Barney, you be better off if'n you git right now 'fore it's . . .' He shivered so hard Barney could see the whole length of him vibrate. 'Oh, law,' he moaned, 'what is I said now! Please, Mist' Barney, don't you go tell 'em I said nothin'!' It burst out like a prayer of fear.

Puzzled, not understanding at all, Barney tried to reassure him. 'I won't tell anybody anything. But I don't see why you think I should leave. Doc's going to help me find my father. That's why I've just got to learn to juggle. But I was wondering, do you think Hoke's method is right? I mean, does it seem to you that a – a – welt across the rear is a good way to make your hands work smoother?'

Billy eyed him a minute and Barney got the odd feeling that

the coloured boy somehow felt sorry for him. Then, with a give-up gesture of his brown hands, he said, 'Jugglin' ain't so hard if'n you think it right. Don't think "catch-an'-throw", think "throw-an'-catch". You got to throw 'fore you catch. Take 'em one at a time.' He turned to start on up the hill.

Barney followed, frowning. It made sense. All at once he realized that Hoke's instructions had only made him clumsier.

'But why would he tell it to me backwards?' he blurted out.

Billy glanced over his shoulder hopelessly. 'Don't you know Hoke likes to use that whip?'

Where the woods began, they separated, each boy taking a different ravine. Barney began to fill his basket with wood, but as he went along his mind was busy trying to sort things. Samson's sarcasm about believing people ... Billy's warning ... and the big black letters: WANTED. He wasn't too sure just what fraud and extortion were, and was thinking about that as he crossed an open meadow ringed round by pines. Suddenly, in the dead grass he saw something white that brought him to a shuddering freeze.

They were scattered a little and it looked like some of them were missing, but there couldn't be any doubt that they were the bones of a man. The scraps of clothing that still clung to them were all that was left of blue denim pants and a red-checkered shirt. Just like any miner would wear. Old bones, half-hidden in the grass for maybe ... a year.

Barney's stomach wriggled inside him, and for a minute he thought he might be sick. He felt a dirty grey all over. Making himself move at last, he circled the skeleton until he saw what he was looking for – the skull, with a small neat hole in it.

The breeze came sharper all at once, rippling the grass that grew round the bones. On the drift of air came the tart sweet smell of chokecherry trees in bloom somewhere. It seemed all wrong, the quiet freshness of the afternoon, the calm of the meadow with the long shadows stretching across it. And then, suddenly the sun dropped behind the rim of western hills and the murmurous forest seemed closed round him, dim and secret, walling him in with this – all that was left of a man, sprawled out in an everlasting attitude of violence, a man unnamed, unmourned, and probably not even known to be dead by his own family. . . . All at once Barney was afraid.

Turning, he ran back down the hill, but he couldn't outrun what he was thinking!

6

BARNEY was dreaming, a nightmare where he was running and dodging – somebody was throwing things at him, at first Indian clubs, and then they changed to bones, white bones. He woke up in a sweat and lay there with his eyes closed, trying to get over the feeling of panic. Huddling in the blankets, he tried to call up the picture of his father, the reassuring smile, the quiet way he always used to talk whenever Barney had awakened, like this, in a fright. But somehow the image of that lean face was blurred and far away. He groaned a little and rolled over.

He was beginning to feel all the sorenesses from the day before, too – his head ached and his arms were stiff, his rear end felt raw. He wondered if Doc might not have saved one bottle of the Curative for emergencies. They had found six more bottles on a back shelf to sell to the crowd last night, but Hoke had stated positively that these were the last. Barney had hated to see them go, though it was none of his business if Doc wanted to be generous and help these stove-in miners.

As he lay there aching and miserable, something nudged him and he opened his eyes to discover that he was being prodded by the strong man's toe. Samson was standing over him, hands on hips, a scornful look on his face.

'You going to lie a-bed all day?' he demanded tauntingly. 'I'd say your pap bred a lazy kid. Probably an easy-living free-loader himself. . . .'

Barney sat bolt up in bed. 'Don't you say anything against my father!'

'What's so precious about him? What's to make you call out in your sleep to him? Is he such a hero? Fancy-dan, maybe? Talks elegant like Doc?' The derision in the words stung Barney worse than Hoke's whip. He scrambled to his knees.

'He's a miner and there's nothing elegant about him, but he speaks decent to people –'

'Oh, that kind? Mealy-mouthed, careful not to give offence or get in any fights.'

'If he was here, he'd razzle you down quick enough!' Barney was on his feet, and before he could stop himself he'd swung a fist at Samson's middle. It was like whaling into a board fence. Where there should have been soft belly, he blunted his knuckles on hard muscle. The strong man was taken by surprise. He stood wordless an instant, then exploded into a sudden blast of laughter.

'Go ahead and laugh,' snarled Barney, pulling on his shoes as fast as he could. 'You're just like Uncle George – you hate people that aren't as big as you.' He flung himself over to where his Mackinaw hung, pulled it down and was almost to the door when the strong man caught him and held on to one arm.

'Barney!' And all at once he was dead serious. 'I wasn't laughing at you. It's just that I could hardly believe – Well, it's the first time anybody ever took a poke at me.' He groped with his other hand, touched the Mackinaw. 'What's this – your coat?'

'You can hold on to me all day, but you'll have to let go sometime. . . .' Barney was past caring what he said in the ragged fury of his anger.

Abruptly loosing his grip on the boy, the strong man stepped back. 'I wouldn't keep you by force, but I'll ask you to stay – for a minute at least – and listen to me.'

The quiet of his tone calmed Barney a little. As he realized what a chance he'd taken, laying into the strongest man in the world, he even felt a weak kind of gratitude that Samson hadn't broken him into little pieces. And then something else occurred to him for the first time – that he had hit a man who couldn't see. It made him go hot with embarrassment. It was the kind of thing his father would have been ashamed of, no matter what the reason for it.

'I'm sorry I punched you,' he said.

'I'm not.' Samson spoke in a straightforward manner now, without the goading mockery. 'I'm glad you did. I had it coming. Nobody's got a right to josh you about something that serious. I don't know what it feels like to be proud of my kin, but if you're willing to fight for your pap, he must be a good man. I shouldn't have made light of him.'

'Then why did you do it?' asked Barney, honestly puzzled.

'I guess I wanted to find out what makes you tick. I thought maybe you were just using your father as an excuse to get sympathy or some trick to wriggle your way into travelling with the Show. I wondered whether maybe the real reason you were staying on here was because you wanted to be a medicine man yourself someday. I thought maybe you were sticking around because you like Hoke and Doc.'

'I do. At least, I like Doc,' said Barney. 'He's treated me kind. He hid me and even lied to save me from getting caught and sent back east. I owe him a lot.'

The strong man walked over and sat down on the bunk, slumping over in that way of his that seemed to be such a habit – elbows on his knees, hands hanging loose. He seemed to be turning something over in his mind, and after a while he nodded, as if accepting a decision that came hard to him.

Raising his head, he said almost humbly, 'Barney, I wouldn't blame you if you walk out of here and don't come back, but I wish you'd stay.'

The appeal had the tight sound of urgency to it, as if it held some importance that went beyond the simple words. And the man who sat and waited for Barney's answer wasn't 'Samson, the strongest man in the world' – he was a tired, sightless fellow named Steve, asking for help.

Slowly Barney went back and hung up his coat. Then he came to stand in front of the man on the bunk.

'Would you show me how to do some exercises?' he asked. And he knew, from the way the dark bearded face twitched and relaxed and almost smiled, that at least this once he'd hit on the right thing to say.

There was a new evenness about their relationship after that. The strong man didn't prod Barney any more. His manner was still blunt enough, but the boy tried to excuse it and didn't lash back at everything. It was an acceptance of each other, if it wasn't exactly understanding – Steve still seemed too remote for Barney to comprehend. He had a way of making strange comments and sometimes stayed silent when a remark was called for. It left the boy convinced that the strong man was, as Doc had said, a little unbalanced in the head, and that made it easier to forgive Steve's abruptness.

In fact, the next day when Doc called him in to run an errand and happened to ask how things were going, Barney was able to answer that he was getting on fine.

'I noticed you've been spending a good deal of time inside the wagon,' remarked the doctor. 'Does Steve talk to you much? Has he said anything about the rest of us?'

'No, sir. Just about how to breathe. He's teaching me some exercises.'

Doc smiled slightly. 'So you've switched professions already, have you?'

Barney squirmed uncomfortably on his seat. 'I don't seem to have much knack for juggling.'

'Hoke says you did well. I believe you hurt his feelings a little, not coming back for more practice. I've told him you will stick with it, though, because of course you realize that you'll make a juggler long before you'll ever be able to lift a thousand pounds. Besides, one strong man with the Show is enough.'

Doc went on then to tell him about the errand – there was a package to be picked up at the printer's, a quarter-mile up the Gulch – but Barney only paid half-attention. He was thinking mostly about Hoke and the whip and wondering how long it would be before he had to try two clubs at a time instead of one.

As luck would have it, he didn't find out – at least not that day. When he went back to tell Steve he was leaving, the strong man took a sudden notion to come along. Of course Barney remembered what Doc had said about responsibilities, but he thought there couldn't be any harm in Steve walking with him a short way up the Gulch and back. Besides, it seemed to mean so much to the strong man.

'I haven't been out of this box for a month,' he said with excitement as he shoved the black flat-crowned hat down on his head. 'No, we don't have to report to Doc, he wouldn't like it. He's afraid if he lets me out of his sight I'll get my hair cut. I did once. Slipped off and found a barber. I hate this mane of mine!' He said it so violently that Barney wondered. He had noticed how the strong man kept his hair clubbed back with that piece of leather round it whenever he wasn't performing in the Show.

'Why doesn't Doc want you to get it cut?' he asked.

'You've seen the act,' snapped Steve. 'Would the effect be the same?'

It wouldn't, of course, but Barney wasn't sure what that had to do with giving medical help to the audience.

'If you don't understand it,' the strong man told him, 'think about it some more.' And that was that.

Feeling somehow as if he'd been caught being stupid, Barney led the way out on to the road. And now for the first time the real fact of Steve's blindness came home to him. Back in the wagon the strong man got around so surely it was easy to forget that he couldn't see, but here on uneven ground he moved haltingly and his hand on the boy's shoulder gripped hard. It wasn't until they had reached the printer's shop that he began to walk a little more easily and take longer steps.

When Barney had collected the package and came out to where the strong man was waiting, Steve said, 'The sun feels good and I'm just beginning to loosen up. Let's walk on a ways.'

It suddenly reminded Barney of Doc's warning that Steve's restlessness might lead to an accident. 'But you', the doctor had added, 'wouldn't let anything like that happen.'

And so he said firmly, 'No, Steve, we'd better go back.'

The strong man's face darkened. 'Doc's orders, eh?' But he shrugged, and they started back without any argument.

'Tried any of the Elixir yet?' asked Steve suddenly. Barney could never get used to the way his thoughts skipped around.

'No,' he said. 'It's so expensive, I didn't like to ask him to give me some, not until I've earned it.'

'You've earned it,' said Steve shortly. 'If I were you, I'd ask for it. After all, if it's got all those rare compounds of nature, including sunlight, minerals, and rare herbs from Ethiopia, you can't afford *not* to take it, can you?'

It was this kind of remark – or at least the odd angry way that

Steve said it – that made Barney question the strong man's mental state, and he was just as glad that he had insisted they go back.

They were almost at camp when he noticed a commotion ahead. A gang of men half blocked the road, clustered round something or someone that Barney couldn't see. The man who was doing the talking was a burly red-headed tough. Whatever he was saying made the others laugh raucously. And then, all at once, they shifted slightly and Barney caught a glimpse of a frightened black face in their midst.

'Steve!' he gasped. 'That's Billy they've got!' He saw the flash of sun off steel – the long vicious blade of a Bowie knife. For a minute he couldn't think. Then, coming out of his shock of fear, he realized Steve was shaking him by the shoulder impatiently, every muscle tensed.

'Snap out of it!' he commanded. 'And tell me how many of them there are.'

'A lot!'

They could hear what the burly man was saying now, his thick voice bragging loud for the benefit of the mob. '. . . and where I come from we don't allow niggers to walk the same street with us white gentlemen. We'd just as lief cut out a coon's gizzard as gut a chicken!'

It was the first time Barney had ever heard mean talk like that, though his dad had told him once that there were a bad lot of folk left over after the war a few years back who blamed the whole rumpus on the coloured people. He wasn't sure just why, but it didn't matter – there couldn't be any good reason for a big bruiser to bully a decent kid like Billy. It stirred up an anger in Barney that helped drive off the fear.

'I'm going to get Doc,' he whispered fiercely. 'Let go, Steve, I've got to run –'

'Don't leave me.' Steve spoke curtly. 'Stop squirming and lead me in close enough to touch the buzzard with the loud mouth. Then get out of the way where I can't hurt you by mistake.'

It seemed a hopeless thing to Barney – a blind man and a boy trying to fight off the whole lot of them. But something commanding in the strong man's confidence made Barney do as he was told. Together they edged into the crowd and worked their way up until they were close behind the redheaded man.

He was holding out the big knife to Billy now. '. . . and I say you're gonna juggle this Arkansaw toothpick or it's gonna lop off your ears, one at a time, right here 'n' now.'

'Please. . . .' There were tears in Billy's eyes as he took unwilling hold of the blade. 'I cain't juggle no sharp-edged knife, mistuh!'

'You hear him?' snickered the redhead. Steve put out a hand, just touching him lightly so that the man didn't even notice. 'This black little devil says he can't juggle. That means he's a fake. And we don't like fakes in this town. We string 'em up to the nearest tree. What did I tell you all about that medicine show? They're a bunch of quacks tryin' to trick you out of your money, usin' fake mind-readin' stunts and freaks. I seen plenty of them kind where I come from! Their medicine's made outa molasses and red pepper. . . .'

Steve shoved Barney behind him with one hand. With the other he reached out, got a grip on the redhead's arm and yanked him round.

'Maybe you think I'm a fake too,' he said. 'Let's see if you're right.' Before the other knew what was happening, the strong man picked him up, easy as a sack of sugar, and pitched him into the midst of the other men, sending them into a tangle of confusion. It all happened so fast that before the mob recovered itself the three of them – Steve in the middle, with Barney and Billy on either side – were hurrying down the Gulch. Barney was trembling with relief, and Billy was sobbing outright, tears streaming down his face.

'I'm mighty obleeged to you, Mist' Steve,' he kept whimpering, 'mighty obleeged!'

'Don't thank me,' growled the strong man. 'It was Barney wanted to save you. What brought you out here? Doc send you looking for us?'

'Yes, suh.' The coloured boy sniffled and put his hands to his face. Then he realized for the first time that he was still clutching the big Bowie knife. 'Oh, law,' he moaned, 'if'n I didn't carry away that man's pigsticker!'

Steve stopped. 'His knife? Where is it?'

Cautiously the coloured boy put it in the strong man's outstretched hand. Steve ran a careful finger across the blade with evident pleasure, then settled the weapon into his belt and buttoned his coat over it. 'If nobody happens to ask about a knife,' he added, 'I don't suppose there's any need for any of us to mention it?'

Quickly Billy said, 'No, suh, I ain't sayin' a word!'

Barney hesitated. 'Suppose somebody does?'

Steve started to say something, but thought better of it. With a short laugh, he said, 'If they ask, then tell 'em the truth. I'd never want you to tell a lie for me. Because if you'd lie *for* me, the time might come when you'd lie *to* me. Now let's go find Doc and tell him to get ready for a clem tonight.'

7

THE doctor was angry. It was the kind of displeasure that pricked Barney the hardest because Doc was silent about it. He listened to what Steve was telling him, but he was looking at Barney with open reproach.

'I got the idea,' finished Steve, 'from the way the big ox was overworking his jaw, that there's a suspicion building up against the Show.'

'Which was not, of course, allayed by your act of violence,' Doc reminded him coldly. 'Townies have a way of not liking to be thrown around. This wouldn't have happened if you'd stayed in camp, Steve.'

'It wouldn't have happened if you hadn't got fidgety and sent Billy to check on us,' retorted the strong man. 'But if it hadn't, you might have found yourself in a clem with no warning.'

Doc glanced at the sun, which was just touching the western ridge of hills. 'It will take an hour or more to break camp. We'll not get out without a brush with them.' He shrugged. 'Billy, go bring up the horses. Barney, tell Maddie we're leaving and help her pack the cooking gear. If Hoke is with her, ask him to come help take down the tent. Steve will stay with me.'

As darkness settled in, everyone was on the hustle, but quietly and with teamwork, as if they'd done this many times. Barney was the only one too jittery to be much help, and finally Doc stationed him on the platform to watch for a crowd to collect. Left standing alone, he strained his eyes to see through the thick dusk, wondering if they'd come in a body or if they'd sneak in quietly, keeping out of sight as long as possible, the way he'd heard the Indians usually did. He jumped at every noise and saw a dozen things that weren't there.

In the quiet he heard snatches of talk – Doc saying, 'All right, Steve, hold tight on that rope!' and a minute later the tent came down with a swish of flapping canvas. He saw Billy crawl across the top of the wagon and pull the tarpaulin over the calliope. He heard Maddie call the poodle to her, just once, sharply: 'Suzette!' The harnesses clanked as the men led the teams in place to hitch up, and it seemed as though they were going to get clean away. When, all at once, Barney saw the townspeople coming.

At first it was only a half-dozen, roaming down the road aimlessly, but their laughter was drunken and charged with the same brash malice that had sounded in the redhead's voice that afternoon. The boy slipped back through the darkness to find the doctor.

'They're coming, but there's only a few.'

By the time he and Doc had got back to the platform, they saw those six and, behind them, a dozen more swaggering along, making remarks in low voices, bracing each other into a dangerous humour. Barney saw one of them tip up a bottle. He wished fervently that he had a gun and thought briefly of Steve's knife. Then, before he could do anything about getting it, the scene was suddenly blazing with light. Doc had touched fire to the kerosene torches. Now Maddie came out behind him in her costume, smiling and gay, carrying in her hands a small eight-sided box with a long bellows that suddenly expanded, letting off a wheeze, and then began to make music as she fingered the pegs on each end. It was nothing to compare with the calliope, but the cheerful reedy melody took the curse off the whispering silence.

Barney, caught by surprise in the middle of the stage, started to duck off, but Doc stopped him.

'No, boy,' he whispered. 'Stay here! When you spot the troublemaker, tell me.'

It wasn't just as Barney had pictured it, his first appearance on the stage. He felt as exposed as an angle-worm turned up to wiggle in bright sunlight. The flares seemed much nearer here, and when he peered beyond the glare, the faces of the men crowding together below him seemed shifty and sinister. Through the sound of Maddie's push-box he could make out their threatening mutter, even caught the words 'fakers' and 'swindlers'.

All at once, from out of the darkness hurtled an empty whisky bottle that sailed past Doc's head and broke against one of the wagons with a shower of glass. Doc seemed not to notice it as he stood there calmly and looked them over.

'Do you see him, Barney?'

The boy made himself peer carefully into the crowd. 'Yes.'

'Don't point!' Doc caught his hand in the very moment he was about to raise it. 'Tell me where he is.'

'About two rows back. The man in the dirty white hat.'

The crowd was growing steadily now, and there could be no least doubt that their mood was a dangerous one. Somebody in front called out, 'Look! They've got their teams hitched!'

And at the same instant Doc spoke up loud enough to drown him out. 'Gentlemen! I give you – our National Anthem.'

He took off his beaver hat. Maddie's push-box began to bring out 'The Star-Spangled Banner'.

Doc nudged Barney sharply. 'Sing!'

'. . . by the dawn's early light . . .' It burst out of Barney so loudly that he even startled himself. The muttering out front dimmed down for a moment, and hats came off grudgingly.

'. . . o'er the land of the free . . . ' Barney's voice cracked on the high note and he rushed on. '. . . and the home of the brave!'

The crowd still jostled and whispered, but it had, for the moment, lost some of its threatening quality. Now Doc stepped to the front edge of the platform, looming over them with his black cape flaring a bit in the night breeze that had sprung up. In a ringing tone to strike awe into the loudest of the roisterers, he said:

'My friends, our errand of mercy to your community is nearly over. Some of you we have helped. A few more may be saved tonight. Since this is my final appearance here – probably the last chance any of you will ever have to find the secret of long life – I have chosen to curtail the joyous spirited free Show which we have donated to your pleasure these past evenings. I had hoped it would provide you with relaxation, but I fear it has actually lulled your hearts into a sense of mistaken security. You seem no longer aware of the deathly fate that awaits you. . . .'

'Quack quack quack!' Somebody made sounds like a duck, and the crowd guffawed.

The redheaded man shouted. 'Let's fit 'im with a Vigilante collar!' And Barney saw that he was waving a rope.

Doc stared down at him, frowning. 'There,' he said, 'speaks a dying man.'

That checked them for a moment. The ones farther back craned to look at the redhead, who tried to swagger it off.

'Don't pay no mind to that slick-tongued buzzard!'

The doctor shook his head pityingly. 'If you think it's just talk, I'm sorry for you, my friend. But I hold no grudge against you for your crude language. In fact, if you have the courage to walk up on to this stage, I will prove your own doom to you.'

Now there was a flurry of small argument down below, men egging the redhead on while he himself was suddenly reluctant.

'You told us these is just fakers,' jibed one of the other men. 'Go on, Red, make 'em prove it!'

So finally the bully climbed up out of the crowd on to the platform, still full of bravado, though Barney thought his grin was only tacked on loosely. Underneath it the man looked uneasy.

'If someone will supply me with a glass of water?' Doc looked out at the crowd. Nobody offered any, though some held up whisky bottles and shouted some coarse remarks about the relative merits of liquor.

So Maddie went into the wagon and brought back some water. All the while Doc looked so awesomely grim that the mob grew oddly quiet. When she handed him the glass, Doc gave it to the redheaded man, then drew from his pocket a metal tube. 'Please put one end of this into the water and blow your breath through it –' He made as if to show him – 'That's the way.'

Smirking and shrugging, the redhead did as he was told, and before the eyes of everyone the water, as it bubbled with his breath, began to turn bright red.

Barney – and everybody else – stared in horrified silence. The glass in the bully's hand began to shake.

'Careful! Careful! Don't spill any of that water!' Doc cried. 'It's highly contaminated now. Here, give it to me and I'll dispose of it in such a way that no one else will become infected.'

The redhead handed him the glass as if it were hot. He

swallowed and scowled. 'It's some sort of rotten trick,' he said unsteadily.

'I wish for your sake it were.' Doc came back wiping his hands with a cloth from which rose a strong odour of disinfectant. 'I'll tell you plainly, sir, that you have osteo-encephalis, a disease which even my Curative cannot touch. The only treatment for it is to rest, avoid talking as much as possible, and try to stay calm. Since it's also highly contagious, I advise you to go home at once and get in bed.'

As the redheaded man stepped down into the crowd, they drew away from him in a panic.

He glowered around. 'You yellow-bellied fools,' he shouted, 'I told you these are tricksters. It's part of their trade – to scare people –'

The mob stood awkward and hesitant. A strong nasal voice was heard to say, 'Watch out who you're callin' a yeller-bellied fewl.'

Before they could rally, Doc spoke up again, as if he hadn't heard or paid any attention to what was going on out front. 'For our final salute to you, gentlemen, our young singer will render a few songs in tribute to our country's fighting men. What shall it be first – "Yankee Doodle" or "Dixie"?'

That diverted their attention all over again. Men began to call out one or the other tune, then began to shout each other down, to turn on each other in angry argument. In just a few seconds they were bellowing, badgering, setting up a clamour of voices that could have been heard a mile. One man swung a fist, and another brought down a whisky bottle with a crack on somebody's skull. In another instant the whole gang was fighting.

'Quick! Hurry, lad!' Doc was pulling Barney back out of the light. They left the platform, left the flares. Hoke and Maddie whipped up their team and led off up the Gulch. As the second wagon pulled away, Barney caught a glimpse of Billy and Steve on the box. Doc stepped over to his own wagon now, helped Barney on to the seat and swung up beside him. He slapped the reins and the team threw their weight into the harness. As they moved away up the road at a lumbering trot, leaving the pack of brawling men behind, Barney began to breathe again. His own part in the business hadn't come home to him yet – he felt as if he'd just watched somebody else having a nightmare. In a daze he sat there until the jolting of the wagon and the night air began to clear his head.

After a while Doc chuckled. 'You can let go of the seat now, boy. It's over.'

Barney unclamped his hands and found that they were aching from the tight grip.

'You did very well,' went on the doctor. 'You came through with good spirit in a tight spot. It's been a long time, but I remember being quite frightened when I first found myself in a clem. As a rule of thumb, you might remind yourself of an old maxim of Indian warfare: knock down the leader with your first shot.'

'Is he – the redheaded man – is he really dying?' Barney was recalling how close he'd been to the man.

Doc didn't seem much concerned. 'We're all dying, lad – in the sense that sooner or later we'll be dead. Unfortunately, that particular type is the healthy, long-lasting variety.'

'But what made the water turn red?'

'I must confess that a bit of magic comes in handy at times. A crystal of chemical in the end of the tube – simple, eh? I trust you'd prefer to outfox a mob rather than try to outrun it?'

And of course Barney was glad they'd got away. He thought

it was a pretty good trick . . . and the redheaded man's words came back to him: 'Trickster'. But, then, if you can't play a trick on a bully, when *can* you?

He turned to Doc. 'And he doesn't have any – you know – osty –?'

'Osteo-encephalis,' the doctor said solemnly, 'is a very real malady, although I believe I'm the first to give it a scientific name. I chose the words from two fine old Latin nouns meaning "bone" and "head".'

Barney put the two of them together and the last of the scare inside him disappeared as he giggled and choked and marvelled at the keenness of Doc's wit.

PART TWO *The Shill*

A decoy – sometimes an innocent fool, but more often a paid carnival hand who sparks the crowd into spending money at the Show

8

'HYA-A-A!' Doc hauled on the reins and the four horses swung left in step together, their big haunch muscles knotting as they dug in and pulled the wagon up the last short steep slope before the valley opened out and levelled off.

Barney roused out of a haze of sleepiness to find that it was daybreak and they were coming into a town – not a scramble of little huts this time, but a double row of well-kept buildings, with other streets beyond, almost filling this little pocket in the mountains. He saw clothing shops, a jewellery store, dry-goods, dressmakers' and milliners' shops – a few saloons, but they were respectable-looking. And then he saw a sign that he recognized with a little tremor. Thexton's blacksmithy – it was here, in a loft room upstairs, that the Vigilantes had organized, they said. It was those second-floor windows that folks used to watch, because when the lights burned at night, it meant the band was going to ride. The little squares of glass were vacant and dark now, though. In fact the whole town lay quiet under the grey dawn.

As they drove along the deserted street, Doc looked around him with open satisfaction. Barney, too, thought this was more like it – the kind of place where he'd expect to find his father. They passed a fine new courthouse building.

'I'll bet they know about Dad in there,' he said.

Doc glanced down at him keenly. 'An excellent idea. I'll make inquiry of them right away.'

A buzz of excitement started inside Barney, at the thought that he might even find his father this very day.

They went straight on through the town and it wasn't until they were almost out into the hills again that the doctor whistled to the wagons up ahead to stop. As they pulled off into a flat open area beside a trickle of a brook, making the same semi-circle as before, the sun was just beginning to touch the tops of the higher hills.

Climbing down, stretching stiffly, the others came over to gather round Doc. He was the only one of them who didn't look sleepy – in fact, there was a briskness in the way he spoke, as if he were pleased.

'As you could all see when we came through the town, this is a progressive community where a lust for gold dust has become refined into a more civilized approach to the gathering of riches. I am so impressed that I believe we'll do well to postpone our Show for today and turn the time to preparation for a gala première tomorrow night. Hoke, you and the boys may brighten the equipment – as quickly as possible, please, since we can expect curiosity lookers as soon as it is discovered that we're here. Steve, please stay indoors today – I want your first entrance to be as effective as possible. Maddie, right now I believe we could all use a spot of tea.'

The men started setting up the tent while Barney helped Maddie get out the cooking-stove and fire it up. It wasn't long before she had the tea brewed and the whole troupe collected to share it. Doc was the last to join them. He had gone in to change clothes and came back looking very fine in a suit of fawn-coloured broadcloth that Barney hadn't seen before.

'One further word before I go to town,' the doctor told them. 'My little diplomatic mission is designed to lay the ground work for good will among the leading townsfolk. I hope to set a mood that may gain us some influential sponsors for our stay here, but it must be handled properly. Therefore, I'm going to ask every one of you to stay strictly in camp, and if any townies come nosing around, let Hoke answer the questions. All understood?'

The sun stood high and bright by the time Doc strolled off down the road, and Barney was having a hard time keeping his eyes open. He led Steve back to their wagon and was about to follow him in when Hoke called him sharply.

'You, Buster! Front and centre! Didn't you hear Doc say there's work to be done?'

With a sigh Barney came back. As he started over to help Billy stake out the horses, the little fat man stopped him. The grin was there, big as a full moon on his face, but Barney was beginning to be wary of it.

'I got other plans for you,' Hoke said pleasantly. 'Bring a couple of buckets of water from the crick yonder. You're gonna wash down the wagons.'

It meant lugging the pails of water up on top of the wagons and sluicing it down the sides, then scrambling around to sponge off the caked dirt and finally doing it all over again for rinse. It wasn't long until Barney was soaked to the skin, but the chill of his wet clothes helped keep him awake, and by noon all three wagons were a brilliant clean red.

Wearily he came back to where Hoke was sitting. Billy had finished with the horses, too – had them curried so their sleek hides glistened in the sunshine. As he came up, along with Barney, Hoke nodded to them both.

'You done real good. Record time. Bill, go catch some sleep. Barney – you ain't through yet.'

Not understanding, Barney protested. 'What do you mean, I'm not through? There's not a spot of dirt –'

'Oh, the wagons *look* all right, but if we was to have to move to a new spot maybe in a hurry, I'd be plumb ashamed of how they sound. The way them wheels screeched last night comin' up the road sounded like a picked chorus of Satan's fiends. You'll find a bucket of axle grease hangin' under the seat of my driver's box.'

Barney stared at him in disbelief. 'But you let Billy –'

'Bill's been workin' a mite harder'n you lately. Practised his Indian clubs ever' day reg'lar. Long as he's got duties t' perform in the bally an' you ain't, you got to expect a few more chores.' Idly Hoke picked the whip up off his belly, where it had been coiled like a sleeping snake.

Barney eyed it, tight with rebellion inside. 'I didn't – even – sit down – once,' he said grimly.

Hoke let the whip ripple out to full length. 'Maybe you're thinkin' I sit around too much m'self. Could that be?' He chuckled. 'Well, I'll tell you – I used to work, too, and then I decided I was a heap too smart fer that, so I quit it and made myself boss. And that there is what makes the difference between me – and you.' With his last word, he flipped his hand, the whip grabbed out and snapped at a sparrow that was picking around the horse tracks. It flopped and fluttered in the dust and then lay still, a little crumple of feathers.

Barney stared at the dead bird. A salty taste came to his mouth and he turned away quickly. Without another word he went over and found the bucket of grease and crawled under the wagon, trying hard not to be sick.

As he worked, he couldn't help spitting, and every time he spit, he looked at Hoke sitting there grinning to himself and blinking in the sun like a fat old toad waiting to swallow a beetle. With afternoon coming on, it was hot under the wagon, and by the time he'd got one wheel packed, Barney was covered with sweat and grease and mud off the bottom boards. He was tired enough to bring tears to his eyes, but every time he slowed down, the whip would mosey over in his direction, knock a fly off the wheel near his head or maybe just snap in the dirt beside him and send a spurt of dust into his face.

And then, through the haze of weariness and rage, he heard Steve call out.

'Hoke, where in tarnation is that lazy kid of mine? He's got chores to do in here!'

It was one straw too many. Sickly, he folded up on the ground and just lay there. Somewhere in the distance he heard them arguing, and then the whip licked across his shoulders and Hoke said grumpily:

'Move! Get on out of there. Go tend your near-sighted friend.'

Barney dragged himself out and stumbled over to the wagon. He tripped over the top step, from pure exhaustion, and almost fell into the arms of the strong man, who waited in the doorway.

'Well, it's about time!' Steve complained loudly, kicking the door shut with a great slam. Then, more quietly he muttered, 'Great Jonah, you stink! Here – go wash yourself. . . .' He piloted the boy over to the stove, where a pail of water was heating. 'Take off your clothes and do it right.'

'I don't care,' Barney roared. 'I don't care whether I stink or not – I don't care – I don't care!' he shouted.

'Well, I do. Use soap.'

Grudgingly the boy scrubbed the grease off himself, dried some of it off and took a mean satisfaction in the smudge it left on the towel. Standing there naked as a peeled apple, he felt even more graceless than when he had clothes on, but Steve couldn't see that.

In a voice as deep with indignation as he could make it, he said, 'I'm not doing any more chores until I've had some sleep.

I'm the only one around here that's done any work, and it isn't fair!'

He stamped across towards his bed, but the strong man caught him, swung him off his feet with an easy hold that pinned his arms, and held him bottom-side-up. 'Did somebody give you a guarantee when you came with the Show that you'd be treated fair?'

Barney struggled weakly, then gave up and hung there.

'You've got a lot to learn,' growled Steve, 'and you're going to need your wits as fresh as possible.' He walked over and dumped the boy on to the bunk, laid a blanket over him. 'Get a good sleep for a change,' he said. 'And that's an order.'

9

IT was barely grey daylight when Barney swam up out of a ten-foot-deep sleep. As he lay listening to the drowsy twitter of the birds and breathed some of the cool fresh smell that drifted in at the window, some sense told him it was dawn – which meant he had slept straight through afternoon, evening, and night without stirring. He scrounged a little in the bed and took pleasure in the comfort of it – under the ticking there was straw, and straw was always good sleeping. Then he remembered whose bed it was and hitched up on his elbow.

Steve was sitting on the floor beside the stove. In the dimness the glow from the banked embers cast a faint ruddy light on the silent, dark-bearded face. His eyes were open and blank, as if he were thinking some far-off thoughts. It gave Barney an odd feeling to suppose that he must have sat there all night.

Rousing out of his musing, Steve seemed to realize that Barney was awake. 'Is it daylight yet?' he asked in a hushed voice.

'Getting to be.' Without quite knowing why, Barney whispered too.

'If you've had your sleep out, then get dressed.' Steve got up and began to patter round the stove while Barney rolled out of the bunk. His own clothes weren't anywhere around; instead, he found laid out a clean pair of overalls and a faded shirt that was long in the sleeves.

'Those are some of Bill's clothes,' added the strong man. 'I gave yours to Maddie to wash.'

It brought home in a rush all Barney's recollections of the day before, and as he buttoned himself up, he began to be angry all over again at the injustice of the way he'd been treated.

Coming over to Steve's side, he said, 'Do you think that the axles had to be greased yesterday?'

'Taste this. Is it hot?'

Barney dipped into the pan of stew that was simmering over the fire. It was good and hot, stirring the boy's hunger. Taking it back to the bunk, he sat down and gulped it, as starved as if he'd just come off fourteen hours of round-up. When he was stuffed and warm inside, he sat back and sighed.

'Thanks for saving my dinner,' he said. 'I'm glad you're not riled at me for not doing any more chores yesterday.'

Steve laughed in that strange way of his that had nothing to do with a thing being funny. 'Is it fairly light yet?'

'The sun'll be up in fifteen-twenty minutes, I'd say.'

'I've a feeling to take another walk,' said the strong man restlessly. 'We'll stay out of town this time so we don't start any trouble – just walk up one of the hillsides. There must be a hill around here.'

'Lots of 'em.' Barney was thinking back uneasily to the sorrowful way Doc had looked at him the last time he'd taken the strong man out of camp.

'Come on, then. I don't want to wait until Doc gets up. He wouldn't let us go.'

'That's what I was thinking,' Barney agreed sombrely.

Steve stopped half-way to the door of the wagon and turned back, his shoulders slanting down suddenly with disappointment.

'Is it so wrong – to want to get shut of this place for a while?' There was a touch of violence mixed with the pleading in his voice as he added, 'Did you know that a small room like this one *sounds* narrow, just as it probably looks narrow? You can feel closed in and shut up –' He broke off and his half-raised hands clenched helplessly in a way that Barney suddenly understood. He himself had felt like slamming his fists against invisible barriers. In one short second he weighed that against his responsibilities.

'All right,' he said quickly. 'I'll leave Doc a note so he won't worry, and we'll stay in sight – he can't get mad at that.'

It took only a minute to find a piece of paper – he felt in the pocket of his Mackinaw and got out the letters his father had written him, stripping the envelope off one. In the bottom of his pocket he found a stub of pencil that he'd been saving, and printed:

WE WENT FOR A WALK UP THE HILL – BACK BY BREAKFAST.
YRS TRULY,

and signed his name in the careful round script his mother had taught him, though it had been a long time since he'd practised it. They left the note on the doorstep of Doc's wagon and made their way quietly across camp, past the horses, and sloshed through the shallow water of the little stream.

Up above, the tops of the hills were beginning to reach up and catch the sunlight, and the sky was full of yellow, although the valley around them was shadowy and quiet.

As they climbed, Steve spoke once, and even though he kept it low, the words sounded very clear in the stillness. 'You said you wrote a note. What does it mean – to write a note? I went blind before I was of an age to learn to write, so I don't have any idea.'

Barney tried to think how to explain. 'Well, you make words out of letters – the same words you'd speak. You say – I mean you spell out on the paper – "We're going for a walk".'

'Is that all there is to it? Then why is a piece of writing thought of so highly?'

'Some papers are proof,' Barney told him. 'Like Uncle George's homestead grant from the government. He keeps that in a locked box. It says the ranch is his, and the President's name is signed to it, which makes it lawful.'

'Suppose you wrote something yourself – suppose you wrote "Hoke is a kind and honest man" and signed your name. Would that make it lawful?'

Barney didn't know whether the strong man was joking or not. He seemed serious enough.

'I'm not anybody,' the boy said, half amused. 'My name doesn't mean anything. If I was President and signed it, that would be different.'

'That would make it true?'

'Well . . . the President wouldn't sign a paper saying Hoke was a nice man.'

They climbed in silence after that, and the edge of the sunlight came sliding down the hillside to meet them. One minute it was grey and cool around them; the next, they had stepped up into warm shining morning. Steve stopped and took off his hat, faced round towards the east and tipped back his head so that the sun fell full on his face.

'That feels good,' he murmured. 'It's a fine thing – to climb and get up somewhere. Level walking gets you into a lazy habit of not picking up your feet. Do you want to rest a while?'

Barney found a flat rock, and they sat down on it, side by side. He was glad enough himself to get away from camp; he had an idea that as soon as Hoke was up, work was going to begin again.

'Steve – do you think I'm lazy?' he demanded.

The strong man shook his head. 'You're a few years young

and a few pounds light to be doing a man's labour. Of course you're going to get tired. Everybody gets tired, but not everybody sticks with it. You've got a good share of stamina for your size. The main thing about work is to see to it the work you do is something to be proud of. Then you don't mind.'

It was straight kind of talk, such as one man might speak to another, and it filled Barney with a respect that he couldn't understand – for, after all, these were just the words of a poor daft blind man and shouldn't be of any account. He had been trying all along to brace himself against caring what Steve said, so it was hardly fitting to take such stock of it now, and yet he'd never felt so grown as he did that minute. Leaning forward with his elbows propped on his knees, hands hanging loose, he looked down into the clearing where the camp was set up. From that height the stream was only a fine blue thread and the horses grazing looked the size of brown beetles. He started to remark about it to Steve, then decided not to.

After a minute, the strong man asked curiously, 'What were you going to say just now?'

'Nothing. It's just that – everything looks different from up here. The clearing's about the size of a dinner plate and the tent looks like somebody dropped a brown handkerchief. The wagons aren't any bigger than salt boxes.' He waited for some sharp sarcastic retort, but Steve only reached down and picked up a little chunk of rock, fingered it thoughtfully.

'If your eyes play tricks on you like that, no wonder it seems to be hard for some people to separate how a thing looks from how it really is.'

'Well, it isn't that I really mix things up! I mean I don't actually think the wagon is only as big as a salt box. I know what size it is.'

'I'm glad of that.' Steve hefted the little stone in his hand.

'Suppose you see a weight with the figure "500 pounds" written on it and suppose you can't pick it up yourself. Would you say that means it really weighs five hundred pounds?'

Barney had to think about that. 'Isn't it, Steve?' he asked. 'Isn't the bar-bell really a thousand pounds?'

'I don't know what it weighs,' said the strong man. 'I can't read.' He rubbed a hand over his eyes wearily. 'All I can do is listen hard and try to figure things out by ear and common sense. I could show you what I mean – you willing to try a new exercise?'

'I'll do anything that'll give me some muscle quick,' answered Barney readily.

'That's not exactly what I meant. It's a different kind of callisthenics, not as easy as push-ups.' Then he said, 'Close your eyes, Barney.'

Puzzled, the boy obeyed and waited. But that was all. It occurred to Barney that this was one of the times he'd just have to humour the strong man, but he decided to do a good job of it, though the minutes dragged slowly and he had to set himself not to fidget. At night when he closed his eyes, he usually went straight off to sleep, but this was different. With every minute he got wider and wider awake. He began to hear things he hadn't noticed before – the stir of wind through the trees up high on the mountains above, though where they sat was quiet as a warm pool. He heard a bird call, but wasn't sure what kind it was, and once he thought he heard something in the grass near by. It was a temptation to look, but he conquered it.

After a while, when he ran out of things to listen to, he began to think back to all that had happened since he'd joined the Show and all at once his curiosity began to prick like a needle.

'Steve,' he said, 'could I ask you a question?'

'I was hoping you would.'

'What's "fraud and extortion"?'

'"Fraud" means fooling somebody. "Extortion" means threatening money out of them.'

'Is it against the law?'

'I don't know much about laws. Laws are no better than the people who make them and the people who enforce them.'

Barney was reminded of the sheriff who robbed stage-coaches, and decided this was true enough. 'But it's wrong, isn't it?'

Steve shrugged. 'It seems to me that deceiving people is a bad thing on the face of it.'

'You know . . .' Barney hesitated to take the strong man in his confidence, and yet he needed to tell somebody. 'You know, Steve, I don't think Hoke and Maddie really read minds.'

'How do you figure that?'

Still with his eyes squeezed tight shut, Barney tried to think exactly what it was that had struck him the other night when he was watching their act. 'Of course, I could be wrong, but it seems to me that every time Hoke looks at somebody's watch or ring, he says something odd that doesn't sound just right. I got to thinking it was some sort of signal, to tell her what the initials are. Like the other night, he said about a silver buckle being "quite a fastening", and right after that she came out with the letters "Q. F." Q is such an odd letter. . . . Anyhow, after that I listened and I was almost sure, and then one of the men in the crowd got the same notion, I guess, because he told Hoke he'd choose an object if Hoke would keep dead-still all the while, and Hoke did and she picked it out anyhow, so I thought I must be wrong. Only . . .'

'Only what?'

'Well, yesterday she was washing, and I saw the blindfol
hanging out on the line, and the sun was coming through it i
two places. They looked like thin places where the materi
was worn through, except they were square. I never saw clot
wear through in square spots. So I wondered if she didn't f
that blindfold so that if Hoke can't speak, he can make signa
with his hands and she can see him.'

Steve clapped an arm across his shoulders so hard tha
Barney's eyes flew open in spite of himself.

'And if their mind-reading act is a hoax, what then?' aske
the strong man with such excitement as Barney had never see
in his face.

'Well, then, I guess . . .' The boy hated to say it, becaus
there was such a smallness about tattling, but then crooke
dealings were a serious thing and couldn't be let to go on. '
guess somebody ought to tell Doc.'

Steve sat silent for a long time. Finally he said, 'What mak
you so sure he doesn't already know? Wouldn't he be a goo
deal of a fool not to know the people who work for him?'

'Not when he's been over in Europe and busy doing all h
scientific experiments all the time.'

'Who told you that?'

'It's in the newspaper clipping – the one I pass round to th
audience every night. It tells about how he's had to travel to g
the compounds, to Ethiopia and Zanzibar. . . .'

'What newspaper said all this?'

'I don't know *which* one, but it doesn't matter. It's a re
newspaper clipping. I've seen a lot of newspapers – they a
look the same, the way they're printed. It's even got h
picture.'

'How does that make it true, though? Somebody had to s

down the words first – maybe somebody about like you or me or Hoke. What's so sacred about a newspaper?'

'It's *printed*.' Barney was beginning to get impatient, because it seemed to him Steve was being deliberately stupid. 'When a thing is printed, it means it's true.'

'Oh.'

Barney began to get suspicious now as he caught a hint of mockery in the strong man's voice, and he thought maybe all this questioning had been to try to make him believe that Doc was a fraud, too. It all went back to what the doctor had warned him – that Steve was hateful of everyone, especially the people who had done the most for him. It seemed a shame to find such ingratitude, but Barney decided to keep his mouth shut about that. Just easily, he said,

'Don't you worry about Doc – if he knew Hoke was a fake, he'd never let him stay with an important scientific outfit like this. So I guess I'd better tell him, because fraud and extortion could get him into trouble.'

'You may be right,' admitted the strong man abruptly. 'And the sooner the better.' He stood up and held out a hand to Barney. 'Come on, let's go back down before he sends out the troops to hunt for us.' He put an arm lightly across the boy's shoulder, and for a minute Barney almost thought it was more than guidance he wanted – there was a needful closeness in the way he held on. Then, fondly, he gave a little shove to start Barney down the hill.

'I guess the fire's lit,' he said, 'even if it does burn slow.'

10

IT was the first time Barney had been in Doc's wagon since they had got to Virginia City. The room was more of a mess than before, cluttered with open boxes everywhere, all full of bottles – Elixir, the Curative. Barney saw with astonishment that Doc had hundreds of bottles of Curative.

The doctor looked up from where he sat in the middle of the tangle, dressed in a shiny silk bathrobe and slippers, drinking tea from a mug.

'Well, what is it, lad? What puts such a look of amazement on your readable young face?'

'I thought you said you'd sold all the Curative!'

'Hardly.' The doctor's lips quirked. 'I'd never allow myself to run out of *that*.'

'But you said – the other night –'

'Oh, I see what you're thinking. It's true, I told the miners below that they were getting the last of it. Makes a man feel good inside to think that he's lucky enough to buy the final bottle. It's part of my approach towards healing – to make people feel good inside.'

'But suppose there was someone else there who really needed it?'

'I'd simply have "found" one more,' the doctor told him agreeably. 'I'd never deprive a poor sufferer of the means of cure.' There was a glint in Doc's eyes that made Barney think he was even more pleased with himself than usual this morning. 'I got your note, lad,' he remarked, 'and, while it was thoughtful of you, I still must insist that you be firm with Steve. Don't let him talk you into leaving camp without telling me first. As a matter of fact, I have a job for you this morning.' Setting aside his cup, he searched in one of the open boxes and brought out a branch of dry juniper wood. 'I want you to help me with something. We've been caught a bit unprepared for such a high degree of culture as we now find ourselves facing. The gentlemen I talked with in town yesterday will not only sanction our stay here, they are even desirous of bringing their good wives to see our little Show. And so –' he handed Barney the wood and a strange-looking tool with rows of teeth like a cheese-grater – 'I want you to sit down on the floor here –' as Barney obeyed, Doc set an empty box in front of him – 'and reduce that dead branch to dust. Just work the rasp back and forth across it and let the filings fall into the box. That's the ticket.'

Barney was puzzled, but this was a good deal better than juggling lessons. Which reminded him of why he had come here!

'Doc, I've got to talk to you about something,' he said. In a burst, he launched into the telling of his suspicions about Hoke and Maddie, at the same time concentrating on the stick with such furious energy that the dust fell into the box in little showers with each stroke of the rasp and a sharp pleasant cedary smell rose from the wood. 'I thought you ought to know before they get you into some sort of trouble,' he finished lamely, and finally risked a glance to see how Doc was taking the news.

The tall man sat watching him thoughtfully, rubbing at his long clean-shaven jaw; he didn't seem surprised. At last he said, 'I appreciate your wanting to keep us from tangling with the law, though I doubt if Hoke and Maddie's harmless little piece of entertainment could ever be found objectionable or illegal. After all, they're not accepting money for their performance – they don't even solicit donations. It all comes under the heading of innocent fun, you see.'

Barney had to admit that was true, but it still seemed wrong to fool people into thinking they could really read minds.

'Did you know about them? About their act being a trick?' He asked it with a disappointment he couldn't hide.

'Of course.' Doc smiled. 'Don't you think I owe it to my little troupe to know each member of it well? As a matter of fact, I will tell you – in confidence, you understand – that there was a time when Hoke and Maddie did have a brief encounter with the law. In such self-righteous cities as Pittsburgh the authorities can be devilish narrow-minded and unfair to two lighthearted entertainers who were only pitting their cleverness against the alertness of the audience. It was then that I was fortunate enough to meet them, at a moment when their fortunes had reached low ebb. Almost in such a way as I chanced to meet you, at a moment of crisis, lad. It has often been my good fortune to be able to help people at the exact right time. Now, there are some who would say you were wrong to run away from home. I don't. I never presume to judge people, nor did I judge Maddie and Hoke. I offered them a job in which they can use their talents to the benefit of mankind, and they've repaid me by being loyal members of my "family". Such as I hope you are. They've spent long hours labouring for the sick and the dying – Why do you wriggle, Barney? Are you not comfortable there?'

'That's not what Hoke said yesterday,' Barney told him unhappily. 'He said he was too smart to do any work.'

Doc stood up abruptly. 'Here, lad, you've done quite enough of that. It's an excellent job, and I thank you. I also want you to know that I've been acting in *your* behalf, wherever the opportunity presented, and I've got definite word that your father did live here for a while, though so far I haven't spoken to anyone who knows where he went when he left.'

The sudden excitement of this news drove everything else out of Barney's head. He scrambled up so fast he almost upset the box of wood dust. 'Who did you talk to? Who knows him?'

'Several gentlemen who own mercantile interests in town remember the name well. They all agree that he dropped out of sight about a year ago.'

'Could I talk to them?' pleaded Barney. 'I want to ask them about him – you know, how he was and how he looked and –'

'I'm afraid they won't be able to tell you much. He must have been a very quiet fellow. Nobody knows anything about him but his name. Of course, if the chance presents itself, I'll be delighted to introduce you to them, but right now we've got to get to work, you and I. I want you to practise a song for me. Tonight, my boy, you join the bally!'

And that news, on top of the word about his father, was almost more than Barney could take all at once. It occurred to him vaguely, later on that day, that there was some question which hadn't been answered, but it didn't seem very important.

'. . . *Be it ev-er so humble, there's no place like home.*'

Barney held on to the last note in fairly good style and was given a round of applause. He felt a glow of pride that could only have been warmer if his father had been standing out in front somewhere to hear him in his first real appearance as part of the bally. He took a small bow, the way Doc had taught him, feeling somewhat awkward in the suit of Billy's that Maddie had cut down to fit him. It was a black silk suit and the handsomest clothing he'd ever had on, makeshift or no. In fact, he felt a good deal better off than Billy just then, since the juggling act had been moved inside the tent. Doc didn't consider it genteel enough for ladies.

In fact, the whole bally had a different tone from beginning to end. The women were all seated, rustling and chirping, in the rows down in front, while the men – a well-dressed, full-fed lot – stood behind and smoked cigars and looked dignified. After the calliope had died down, Hoke had stepped on to the new platform that he and Doc had built to take the place of the one left down the Gulch, and he'd made a little speech of welcome. Then Maddie did the mind-reading act without any catch-words this time, and Hoke was so good at signalling with his hands that Barney couldn't even discover most of the movements, though he did finally decide that rubbing one eye meant 'a watch' and a finger run round his collar meant 'a ring'. After that, the poodle dog, Suzette, did some cunning tricks, ending by saying her prayers, which made the audience clap, and finally Doc came on and spoke to them. He said he had some important things to tell them, but first they'd hear a song from the famous young concert artist who had sung before the crowned heads of Europe *and* the Continent. This was such a surprise to Barney that he had a hard time getting the first note out, though after a few bars he settled down. And now, as the applause faded out, Hoke was inviting the gents inside the tent for some man-talk and Doc allowed that he'd give a little travel lecture to the ladies.

It was all about the Egyptians, for some reason, and while he spoke Barney was stationed to one side of the platform holding up a picture, a big fine painting of the pyramids and the sphinx and a camel in the foreground.

'Yes, ladies, these are the pyramids,' Doc was explaining.

'The tombs in which the Egyptians buried their beautiful young princesses, whose lifeless bodies lie entombed to this very day in a perfect state of preservation. From these sacred walls, the few of us who have learned to decipher their hiero-glyphics have unravelled the secrets of their intricate magic formulas, the amazing recipes that had never been rediscovered since the mysterious elegance of the reign of Cleopatra. Of course, to find the rare herbs and roots and berries of which they are compounded, I had to journey to the headwaters of the Nile, where it rises in the mountains of darkest Africa. Thus, after years of experimentation, I have managed to achieve the very essence which the proud queens of Karnak used to sur-round themselves with irresistible fragrance. Can you imagine such a princess allowing any distasteful scent to mar the cool aromatic vistas of her palace? Whether the subtle human odours or the noxious vegetable aromas, the insidious smell of cook-eries. . . .'

This struck Barney as a little far-fetched. He'd always thought the smell of food was good. Frying onions made his mouth water just to think of them. But the women in the audience were all nodding to each other as if they agreed with Doc that such things were terrible.

'And so, with an amulet of this incense, the Egyptians kept their air pure as that of a virgin pine forest. The priestess burned it in her temple; the beautiful wife, no less a priestess in her own right, was never without the perfume of it in her – boudoir.' He spoke the word delicately, and the ladies rustled and tittered.

'To you, my dears, I offer this incomparable magic!' Doc opened a small silver box in which there were a number of pieces of something wrapped in a shiny silver paper. 'Just breathe the delicate fragrance. . . .' He unwrapped one piece and handed it down to a lady in the front row. Almost unbelieving, Barney saw what it was. Saw it? He *smelled* it! And it was a good thing Doc's back was turned to him; for a minute the boy was shocked speechless. Because the magic incense of Egypt was nothing more than the wood dust that he himself had filed that morning, mixed with something to harden it into a pellet. There was some other perfume added to it, something like peppermint, but mostly the smell was plain cedar.

'Isn't that essence marvellous?' Doc demanded warmly. 'Beg pardon? Oh, the price? In appreciation of the heart-warming welcome you have extended us upon this first visit of ours to your handsome community, and as a special favour to this particularly fair audience, I will let go these incomparable buds of magic fragrance for a fraction of their real worth. I will sacrifice them at the token price of one dollar.' He held them out to the ladies.

There was a good deal of stirring around as purses were got out and silver eagles began to jingle. In a rigid sort of amazement, Barney counted thirty or more dollars that the doctor took in on the product of one dead stick of juniper that anybody could have found around the hills.

Steve's words kept coming back to him, about being proud of your work. More than that, he kept getting a picture in his mind, clearer than for a long time, of his father's plain straight face, and he knew what his dad would think of this foolery.

Finally the townsfolk were smiling and saying 'Good evening' and 'Lovely performance' and 'Charming!' and all that. As they were getting ready to stroll back towards town under the brilliant full moon, Barney suddenly got a notion to ask some of them if they knew where John Morgan might have gone. The Show was over now, Doc couldn't mind. He jumped down off the platform and was almost into the crowd when a firm hand reached from behind and caught him – gently but strongly held him back. He turned and looked up into the grey pointed face of the doctor.

'Easy, lad,' he murmured.

'But I just thought I'd talk to somebody –'

Doc led him away from the others. Quietly he said, 'I'd thought to shield you from the sad truth, at least for one more night, but now I see that I must tell you the worst.'

There was a black velvet sadness in his whispered tone that made Barney go cold with premonition. 'What worst?' he asked shakily.

'I'm sorry to be the one to inform you that your father – is dead.'

11

BARNEY hadn't cried in a long time – it didn't come easy but wrung itself out slow and cramped his innards into a tight twist of grief. Bunched up on his bedding in the corner of the darkened wagon, he tried not to make any noise, but sometimes his clenched throat almost choked him and his breath came in long shaky gasps.

After a while, out of the darkness from over where the bunk was, Steve spoke in his usual hard matter-of-fact way.

'Go ahead and cry out loud. It hurts more when you try to hold it in.'

If there was one thing he couldn't take, Barney thought, it was any of Steve's prodding. Uncurling out of his huddle, he groped his way over to the door, but the strong man heard him and got up, found his way through the darkness quicker than Barney could, and caught him by the shoulder before he could get out.

'Done it again!' he muttered to himself. 'I seem always to send you running from me. Now wait a minute. . . .' Firmly he led the boy back to the bunk and made him sit down. 'Trouble with me is, I usually bust out with the truth and most people don't like to hear it. I wasn't mocking you, Barney – I meant just what I said. It's easier and gets over with quicker if you let it come out, out loud. I ought to know. I've lain right here in this bunk and cried too.'

That shocked Barney out of thinking about himself for a minute. 'Did your father get killed?' he mumbled miserably.

'My father sold me for fifty dollars cash. But that wasn't why I cried. It's a long story. Right now we've got your problems to try to work out.' The steady confident sound of the words and the way Steve said 'we' roused Barney out of the tight paralysis of his sorrow, and he began to breathe a little easier.

'What is there to work out?' he asked painfully.

'Where was your father supposed to have been killed?'

'I don't know,' Barney said. 'Doc just told me he got shot.'

'Did you talk to the man who told Doc?'

'No. Doc said it would only make me feel worse.' Barney's voice was beginning to get raspy again. 'He said Dad wasn't very well liked around here.'

'Did he tell you where your father is buried?'

'I didn't ask him. Maybe they just – There's a lot of bones lying around these hills,' he mumbled painfully.

'That might be true, if a man gets dry-gulched and nobody knows of it. But if people know of it, they bury him and make a record of it.' He gripped Barney's arm now, with a rough urgency. 'You can't afford to take *anybody's* word on something this important. You've got to make sure!'

'But why would the man lie about my father?'

'He could have been mistaken.'

'Doc said he was sure.' And then it broke across Barney like a sudden fever. 'Do you think *Doc* could have –?'

'What do you think?'

'I think – I think – Well, I *know* the medicine isn't real. That incense. . . .' He went on to tell Steve about the juniper branch. 'And that made me think back to what the miner said about the Curative being just molasses and red pepper, and I remembered I saw some big jars of peppers and molasses in Doc's wagon, and something called Hartshorn. . . .'

'That's a kind of salts, to make a poor sucker think he's had a dose of something,' commented Steve. 'Go on.'

'So I figured that Doc is a fraud, too, like Hoke and Maddie, and that's why he lets them stay with the Show, but why would he tell me a lie about Dad? He's always treated me kind. Why would he want to fool me about a terrible thing like that?'

With a strained sort of patience, Steve said, 'Do you really feel he's done you such a big favour, giving you a few skimpy meals and a bed on the floor, in return for which you work from sun-up until after dark? Do you know what it would cost him to hire a man to do the chores that you and Billy do, plus a couple of extra acts for the Show – even if he could find somebody willing to travel all over tarnation, sometimes with a mob on their tail? Think, Barney. Think!'

'Think?' He shook his head rebelliously, trying to shake clear the muddle of thoughts that were already there. 'I'm all mixed up. Why do you always tell me to think?'

'Because,' said Steve grimly, 'it's your only hope.' And then he added, 'And mine, too.'

Barney was awake more than he was asleep that night. About the time the window began to show grey, he heard Steve come over and squat down on the floor at his side.

'Did you figure out what to do?' he asked.

'I'm going to slip on in town before anybody's awake to stop me. I've got to talk to somebody, I guess.'

'Where will you begin?'

'There's a court-house we passed on the way through town.'

'Good. Start there. If they don't have a record of his death, then he's probably still alive, so ask in places where people come and go – the barbershops and eating places, maybe at the hotel.'

Barney finished lacing up his boots, got up and went over to get his Mackinaw, although the morning was muggy and warm.

The strong man, following him, reached out and touched the heavy coat lightly with his fingers. 'You're not coming back?'

The boy didn't want to answer that. He kept telling himself he didn't know what he was going to do. 'I'm just taking the coat because it's raining,' he said.

Steve was silent a minute, then he let out his breath in a long sigh. 'You'll be in a man's world, Barney. Sometimes anybody, no matter how much muscle he's got, runs up against something too big to meet head-on. If you find yourself coming to something like that, don't get mad and throw yourself against it. You're apt to get busted up. Have enough patience to figure out a way over it or round it – and don't be ashamed to ask for help.'

Hardly knowing why the recollection should come back to him now, Barney said, 'Doc told me once you hated to be helped.'

'Doc says a lot of things, doesn't he?' Steve shrugged and turned away. 'Good luck.'

12

As Barney walked down the road towards town, he'd never felt more lonesome in his whole life. The rain spattered in his face, and he thought dimly how Aunt Norah would have jumped on him for slogging along in weather like this, kicking up mud on his boots. For a minute he was even homesick for her scolding.

He kept thinking of Steve, too, and thought he would probably miss the strong man's curious humour. All the odd things Steve had been saying these past days, things that Barney had put down to his being butter-brained, now began to seem to point in a sort of direction, even though the boy still wasn't sure what they meant. One thing he did know: that talk of Doc's about Steve being addled was just another lie. The strong man had known all along that the medicine was no good, and that was why he hated Doc. But then Barney couldn't help wondering why Steve stayed with the Show, unless – it was because he was blind and couldn't get away. That idea hadn't occurred to him before. He could almost hear Steve pleading with him to *think, Barney, think*.

And then a cheerful voice broke in on his pondering. 'Hey there, sonny, ain't it some damp out there?'

It was a group of men standing together under a tarpaulin slung between a couple of trees. They were gathered round a fire that was burning in an old tin drum.

Another one called out, 'Come on over here, soldier, and put something hot in your belly.' And Barney saw they had a pot of coffee on to boil.

The rain had sprung one of those heavy spurts just then, and Barney was glad to go over and get under the tarpaulin for a minute. He took the cup they handed him and enjoyed the hot tang of the drink.

'This ain't hardly no day for strollin',' one of the men remarked.

Barney glanced around at them – all workmen, dressed in overalls and heavy boots. Their curiosity seemed to have no meanness in it, so he answered up, told them he was looking for word of his father. They listened, but shook their heads.

'Afraid we can't help none on a thing like that,' one said. 'We ain't from around here – we're Western Union.' And when they saw he didn't know what that was, another one explained. 'We put up the telegraph line.' He pointed to a pole near by, a plain peeled log set upright in the ground with a crossbar on top and some long coils looping down from it. 'We just put through a line from here to Helena. Now we're startin' a new one across to Bozeman.'

'What for?' asked Barney.

'Well, now, so's folks can send messages. That there copper wire, strung to them poles, transmits an electrical signal, so's a man in St Joe, Missouri, can tap the key in code and a man on t'other end in Denver can read it.'

'You mean you can just tap one end of a wire and –'

'Not just any wire, soldier, *copper* wire. Got to be copper. That's what they call a good conductor.'

'Could you even send a message to Pittsburgh?'

'Pittsburgh – Californey – one of these days the whole blinkin' country's gonna be criss-crossed with telegraph lines to where you can't get out a sight of 'em.'

Barney thanked them and went on towards town, feeling a little better after a few friendly words and a hot drink.

At the court-house the clerk listened to his question with a flat sleepy boredom that some older people get when they listen to kids. 'Don't recall any buryin' by that name,' he grumped.

Holding his breath almost painfully, Barney waited while the man ran an ink-stained finger down the pages of his record ledger. Finally shook his head. 'Ain't here. Leastwise, not in the last year.'

So now, with his hopes on the simmer, Barney went back outside and even the rainy sky looked better to him. He stood on the corner a minute, trying to think where to ask next – the barbershop, Steve had said. He saw a striped pole down the street.

The barber was cocked back in a chair by the front window with his feet up on the sill, reading a copy of the *Madisonian*. He eyed Barney sourly, but when he heard the name John Morgan, his face unstiffened.

'Are you his boy?' Then he nodded. 'Yep, you look some like him, I can see that. No, I ain't seen him around for quite a spell. Reckon he's left town. Weren't specially popular with some folks. Always was fair-spoken to me, though. You might ask at the Virginia Stables. He used to keep his horse there.'

The stable was on a back street at the far end of town. It was a good place to come in out of the rain, full of the smell of hay and horses and leather and grain, quiet except for the drum of the rain on the tin roof high over the loft. The stableman was busy sweeping out.

'If you want to know about John Morgan, ask old Skinner.' He jerked his head towards the back room, where Barney could see a white-haired burly-faced man sitting in front of a pot-bellied stove. He blinked and teetered idly on the two back legs of his chair and didn't see Barney at first, until the boy shuffled a little and stirred him out of his musing.

'John?' The watery blue eyes peered up sharp and warm at the question. 'You're John's boy? You're Barney? Tarnation! The times he's talked about you! Here, set down. Where'd you drop from?'

It brought a flood of relief, like meeting an old friend. Not wasting any time on his own history, Barney began to pump out the questions, and the old man tried to answer.

'John Morgan was the best friend I ever had. Killed? Who told you that? They run him out of town, but they daren't kill him. Well, now, I shouldn't of said "run" – he took his good time goin'. Stopped to say good-bye to me and the missus. Y'see, my missus been sick these last two years – stommick ailment. Pill-roller says she's a goner if she don't eat exackly right – got her on a diet of eggs an' milk. And John, your pap, John used to go clear down to the ranches along the Big Hole and bring back fresh eggs fer us when the supplies run short here, winter 'fore last. I tell you, if it weren't fer him, the missus might've died. Me, I'm too old to ride, myself. I miss that father of yours, boy. Town lost a good man when he left.'

It made Barney burn with pride inside, but he couldn't help asking, 'Why did they run him out of here?'

'Well, your pap's a different breed from these tramp miners. With him it's a trade, an' he takes a pride in it. Told me once, a Welshman's part hardrock and part hot steel. Anyhow, he liked to work, and that makes folks suspicious of a man. He come here late, after most of the good panning ground along the Gulch was already took, an' 'stead of jumpin' somebody's claim, like another man would, he went up one of the smaller cricks and staked out his claim back in the hills. It was smaller pickin's, but, like I say, he's a hard worker; panned out a livin', which give folks the idee he must've found a rich spot. So what happens? Naturally, a big lazy gunny, fairly popular citizen of this here vicinity, decides to move in on your pap's claim, by right of two Colt forty-fives.'

'But isn't there a law against that?' Barney demanded.

'Well, there's a court, yes, there is. And your pap took the matter to 'em. Only, somehow they decided the whole business was, what you might say, outside their jurisdiction.'

'Did my father have a gun?'

'Sonny, your pap don't hold with guns. He says it ain't no way for lawful folk to settle things – too many innocent by-standers get messed up by them low-flyin' black ducks. What's them? Them's bullets, sonny. What he done, though – your pap, that is – one night he met the big sidewinder and took him on barehanded. Your pap ain't a big man, but he makes up fer it with ginger. Left that gunny stretched out, colder'n a banker's heart.'

'And he got his claim back!'

'Well, not exackly. You see, these here careful people we got runnin' our town, all they could think of was how your pap was askin' to git hisself murdered, maybe in front of one of their purty shops, so they called him a troublemaker and in-vited him to git. Easier to do that than to ask the big gunny to leave. Lots safer, too.' He spat towards the stove in disgust. 'Yes, sir, sonny, your pap told me he weren't sorry to go. A man's got to have faith in his neighbours, that they got the gumption to stand up fer what's right.'

'Did he tell you where he was going?' Barney asked urgently.

Skinner shook his head. 'All he said was, he might try a new camp over t'other side of the divide. It ain't much shucks fer gold, but they're diggin' a little silver there, puttin' down shafts fer it. Your pap said that kind of minin' is more his style.'

'What's the name of it and how far is it?'

'Place called Butte, over on the Silver Bow River. I never

been there, but it's just the other side of Pipestone Pass, three-four days' ride north and west, they say.' The old man shook his head. 'I hope you find him, boy, and when you do, give him this. . . .' He dug into a pocket and pulled out a little smooth rock, a dull yellow-coloured bit of stone – except that it wasn't. When Barney took it in his hand, he realized it was metal.

'Don't know what it is?' The old man chuckled. 'That's gold, sonny. That's a nugget, worth maybe twenty dollars in cash at the Wells Fargo office – more'n that in trade. Hang on to it and give it to your pap when you see him. Tell him old Skinner had a good day pannin' and wanted to remember him.'

Barney felt a little embarrassed to take the nugget, but since the old man put it that way, he couldn't refuse. 'Thank you,' he said. 'I'll tell him what you said.'

'Tell him I said this town's a worse place without him. Gettin' so civilized, folks forgot the strong and the weak of things. Only they ain't, really. They ain't forgot, they just lost their spunk. That's what the Vigilantes done fer us.'

'I've heard of them,' Barney said soberly. 'But didn't they clean up the town? Wasn't that a good thing?'

'Good. I dunno. They meant it good, I reckon, and they made the place quieten down. But this ain't a proud quiet – not when a string of numbers can shiver folks in their beds. Numbers don't mean nothin' – just a scare sign, like the old skull-and-bones. Trouble is, anybody kin write 'em. Been a long time since the old days when the Vigilantes held trials – they thought they could handle it fair when they took the law in their own hands. Never figgered how they'd started somethin' they couldn't turn off. Well, they found out. If one man kin call hisself a Vigilante, so can another. Only now there ain't no trials no more, sonny. Death comes whoopin' in under cover of night to strike down good men, just out of some spite or other, and call it "justice". What good is justice if it don't pertect a man like John Morgan? You want to know why the court didn't uphold your pap's claim, sonny? It was on account of the night before they was to decide, every man jack of 'em found the numbers writ on his door. The black 3–7–77. That's why a self-respectin' man ain't gonna live here. I'd leave, too, if the missus wasn't so tarnation sick – What ails you, sonny?'

Barney didn't answer – he couldn't. He'd just looked up to see Doc standing in the doorway.

'Well, well,' the tall man said pleasantly. 'They told me I'd find you here, Barney.' He stepped into the small room and bowed to old Skinner, as polite as if he were greeting the Mayor. 'I've been looking all over for you, lad, I have news for you – about your father.'

'What news?' Barney was suspicious of anything that Doc might say now, and yet he couldn't afford not to listen.

'It's rather private. I think we'd better postpone it until later. Aren't you going to introduce me to your friend?'

Unhappily the boy obeyed. Old Skinner seemed surprised and flattered when he heard who Doc was. And when the doctor unbuttoned his slicker, which fell open to show the fine clothes underneath, the old man really was impressed.

'You're the feller runs the medicine show up yonder?' he said. 'Ever'body says that's a whackin' good show you put on. I ain't been up to see it yet.'

'We try to spread a little pleasure with our performances,' admitted Doc modestly, 'but our real mission is the healing of the sick. Did I hear you say your wife is ill?'

'Been troubled for three years – like she got a hot brick down in her stommick every time she eats anything. . . .' The old man went on to describe symptoms while Doc listened and nodded gravely.

At last Doc said, 'It's fortunate that we've met, sir. It so happens that I have a Curative which works miracles for complaints of the stomach. It's a blend of rare ingredients from Tierra del Fuego, where stomach trouble is absolutely unknown to the natives. I went on an expedition there last year just to gather the bark of a certain tree. . . .'

As he was talking and the old man was beginning to look interested, Barney was thinking – of a sick woman who could only eat eggs and milk, and of the Curative that had made many a healthy miner choke.

All at once he burst out, 'No! It's not so, Mr Skinner. His medicine's a fake – it's almighty bitter and full of red pepper –'

Doc was seized by a sudden coughing spell that drowned out what Barney was saying, but Skinner shot the boy a quick look. His blue eyes squinted up, and far back in them there was a sudden gleam of understanding.

When Doc had recovered from his choking fit, he said lightly, 'Barney's joking, of course. He's got a fine sense of humour. We're always teasing each other, aren't we, lad?'

Skinner nodded. 'I can see that. It's a good joke, too. As fer your medicine, sir, I'm sure it's dandy, but you see the missus sets a lot of store by her own pill-roller and I reckon she'll want to stick with him and his diet. You know how wimminfolk are.'

Doc smiled and bowed and seemed glad to be leaving. As he reached the door, he beckoned to Barney. The boy hesitated. He wanted no more of Doc and the Show, and after his outburst he was even a little afraid of what Doc might do. Yet, he figured, he was faster afoot than an older man, and besides, there was the off chance that Doc really did have news of his father. So, saying a hasty 'good-bye' to Skinner, he followed at a safe distance, ready to cut and run the first time Doc made a move towards him.

But when they reached the street, Doc only smiled, a little hurt. 'That wasn't very kind of you, lad, to try to arouse Mr Skinner's suspicions of me, but I'm sure you didn't mean any harm. Come, now, we have no time to waste.' And he started off at a brisk pace, the slicker flapping open about his knees. The rain had stopped altogether, and the air was warm and damp as the sun tried to break through the low-lying mist.

Barney kept a few steps behind, still ready to dodge if necessary, as they walked up the back street and out on to the road to camp. When they passed the Western Union workers, Barney saw that they were busy setting a new pole; they waved and Doc waved back to them, so Barney knew how his steps had been traced into town.

As they went along, Doc was saying, 'My informants told me wrong yesterday. Your father wasn't killed around here, as was reported. But, then, I suppose you found that out this morning?'

Barney didn't answer.

When they got back to camp, Doc led the way straight over to his own wagon and went in, with such imperative haste that Barney forgot his caution and followed curiously. The wagon was dim at best; on a grey day, it was even darker inside. He stopped just within the doorway, and then, so quickly that he hardly knew what had happened, Doc had him by the arm, thrust him in, shut the door and locked it. And Barney knew that once more he'd been fooled.

13

Doc lit the lantern on his desk and sat down. As he looked at Barney, the kindliness was gone from his face at a stroke, leaving it bleak and cruel. When he spoke, his voice was as thin as the cutting edge of a knife, and as deadly.

'Come here.' And this time he didn't point to the chair beside the desk, but motioned the boy to come and stand in front of him.

For a split second Barney felt a stir of terror – an impulse to refuse, to resist and fight a fight he knew he couldn't win. And then Steve's words came back to him. Something too big to meet head-on ... don't get mad and throw yourself against it ... figure a way over it or round it. Slowly he walked forward and stood in front of Doc, meeting the cold look of the pale grey eyes as steadily as he could. He was wondering how he had ever come to think of this man as a friend.

'Now, then, I want to know who put you up to this – telling people that the medicine isn't genuine, trying to stir up trouble. Did Steve –'

'I found it out myself. I heard the redheaded miner say it was only molasses and red pepper, and I saw those things right there in your cupboard.' Barney pointed at it. 'That old man's wife might have died if she ate the wrong thing. But that wasn't what I went to town for – to tell people about the medicine.' Bluffly he demanded, 'What news do you have of my father?'

Doc eyed him hard. Then, all at once, the grimness changed

and he put on a sorrowful look which Barney recognized now for just another piece of play-acting. He felt stronger for the knowledge.

'I was going to tell you some of the details surrounding his death. I have now talked to a man who actually witnessed it.'

That jolted Barney, and he had to remind himself that this was probably another lie, but he held fast to his new-found courage.

'As I told you,' Doc went on, 'your father did not die here in Virginia City. He left a year ago to go west to Oregon. Somewhere on the way, some little town without a name, he got into a gunfight – apparently he didn't draw fast enough. Most unfortunate. I grieve for you, lad.' He shook his head gloomily, but secretly he was probing with the narrow pallid eyes. 'You don't believe me, do you?' he said after a minute.

Barney didn't answer.

'You're very young, my boy,' said Doc, leaning back in his chair. 'A good deal too young to pass judgement on your elders. I gave you credit for some maturity when we met, but now I see that your impulsive nature and instability are still in a childish state of uncontrol. It's fortunate for you that you happen to be with us at this unhappy time. I want you to know that I will forgive your breach of loyalty – I want to be your friend. I want you to trust me in all things, I want to be like a second father to you in these formative years.'

'Why?' asked Barney bluntly.

'Because it's the only humane thing to do. My conscience would prick me if I thought of you wandering this savage country alone, friendless, too young to fend for yourself.

You'd probably end up in an orphanage, and, from what I hear, that's a highly unpleasant fate.' And Doc feigned a slight shudder.

Barney had heard a few things about them himself, but he wasn't ready to admit he was an orphan. 'Thank you,' he said as politely as he could, 'but I'll get along all right.'

'Tut-tut, lad, you're fidgeting. Here, let me give you something to settle your nerves. . . .' Doc reached into the cupboard and took out the red box which Barney had noticed there once before. Opening it, he picked out a chunk of some dry stuff. 'Chew on this. Go ahead – taste it. It's nothing but a mixture of paraffin and chickle. Haven't you ever seen chewing gum before?' he said, pushing it into Barney's hand.

It was new to Barney, but it smelled and tasted faintly sweet, and as he chewed, it worked down into a rubbery wad that wasn't unpleasant, although it made quite a jawful.

Meanwhile, Doc was talking on crisply. 'You don't know how difficult life can be for a boy your age. You're too young to be given a man's work and you're too old to be taken into someone's home as a foundling. No, son, your best bet is to stay with the Show. Once you've got the swing of it, it may even make you rich some day. For instance . . .' He reached into a drawer of the desk and brought out a printed paper, handed it across. It was a copy of another newspaper clipping with the same picture of Doc on it and headlines that read: CATHCART LEAVES FOR MONTANA TERRITORY ON MISSION OF MERCY. Barney read the first paragraphs with growing wonder.

Dr Primus D. Cathcart, world-renowned scientist, has been commissioned by the International Society of Medicine to go to the Territory of Montana on an errand of mercy, it being well known that the entire population of that vast area suffers from incipient weakness, caused by inhaling the pollen of the loco weed, a native plant which causes animals to go insane and which, when its pollen is breathed, produces a form of inertia in human beings, diluting their strength and especially sapping the virility.

To cure this complaint, Dr Cathcart has perfected a Curative with miraculous restorative powers which it derives from its ingredients, certain rich grasses which grow along the Siberian Steppes, of a type much like the American 'bunch' grass, although a hundred times more strengthening, so full of latent energies that it has been known to cause domesticated stallions to revert to their original wild state. Through long experimentation, Dr Cathcart has made a distillation of the miraculous essence of these grasses, converting it into a form which human beings can assimilate. . . .

Barney didn't know whether to laugh or get angry. 'Who wrote this?' he demanded, almost unbelievingly.

'I did, of course, using the valuable material you supplied me with on that first ride of ours.' The doctor seemed amused.

'But what newspaper printed it?'

'Does it have to come from a newspaper to be set in news type? An obliging young printer down in the string-town ran it off for me. He wasn't bright, but he did know how to lay out a column. In fact, I believe you even picked up the package for me. So, you see, you deserve a good deal of the credit for our newest piece of literature, and because I believe in paying for what I get, I'm going to show you how brainwork can make money.' Doc put a brand-new dollar on the table. 'There you are, lad. Your first cash earnings.'

It was the sight of the silver that did it. Up to then Barney half thought it a joke. But he'd seen pieces of silver changing hands every night, silver hard earned by miners' sweat, paid out for 'medicine' that was no more made of grass from Siberia than it was made of berries from Ethiopia. All at once, he wouldn't have touched that money for all the gold in Alder Gulch.

Steadily he said, 'I don't want to help you sell fake medicine. I don't care what you pay me, I don't want to stay with the Show.'

The smile slipped from Doc's face as if he'd pulled off a mask. 'Like that, eh?' he said very quietly. 'Now I will tell you what it will be, whether you like it or not. You are a well-favoured young man with an open and beguiling face, an innocent manner and a voice that is clean and pure. I intend to train you to be of use to me – as has been my plan from the beginning. You will be a roustabout, a performer, above all, a shill; with your air of unimpeachable honesty, you will learn to stand among the crowds, nightly, and give personal witness as to the merits of the Curative. Meanwhile, you will go on with your juggling practice and you will learn certain other arts and crafts connected with our trade – oh, yes, you will. There are many ways to convince stubborn boys, and I'm fairly well practised in all of them. Steve apparently has learned his lesson. So has Billy. . . .'

The way Doc talked on in that monotone struck a coldness through Barney. By the very lack of excitement, it made the threat of what he was saying seem ordinary and inevitable.

'In your case,' he went on, 'I hope I'll be able to preserve your charm intact, at the same time teaching you obedience through reason. I believe you have a good head on you. I think I can convince you, for instance, that this business of your referring to the medicine as "fake" must stop. To do it, I'm going to prove to you that this cabinet of mine contains many things which you have not seen yet.' He leaned back and reached far into the cupboard to bring out a bottle. 'Perhaps you can tell me whether this is medicine or not – you are the expert.'

The liquid looked clear as water, but the minute Doc unscrewed the cap Barney recognized the strong unpleasant smell of castor oil. He watched in growing discomfort as Doc took out a glass and poured it clear full.

'Since this isn't medicine,' said Doc, 'it won't affect you. Of course, if it *were*, it would be a rather large dose, might make you uncomfortable, even a bit sick. But then you've said my medicine is "fake", so you won't mind drinking it.' He held it out, the narrow face mocking and merciless.

Barney backed off a few steps. 'I know what it is,' he muttered. He wasn't sure how Doc could make him drink it, but he had to admit that, one way or another, he probably could. 'How . . . how will I do my chores if I get sick?' he asked.

The tall man chuckled dryly. 'Oh, so we're keen for our chores now, after so nearly quitting the Show a moment ago. Well, well, I believe your training will come along fine. I hope you won't forget your enthusiasm as soon as you're outside my door.'

As soon as I'm outside your door, vowed Barney mentally, *you won't see me again!*

'So, to impress our agreement on your mind, I'll settle for a compromise. That chewing gum of yours has probably lost its flavour by now. Suppose you bring it here and revitalize it – in this.' Doc held out the castor oil again, adding sharply, 'Come, boy! I'm letting you off easy. Don't hesitate or I may change my mind.'

And this time Barney knew the doctor meant what he said. Stiffly he stepped forward, took the gum out of his mouth and dipped it in the oil. The first thick greasy taste made him nearly vomit, and the ill-flavoured wad seemed to get bigger as he chewed, but he set his face not to show his disgust.

Leaving him standing there, Doc turned away, got out a piece of very handsome paper, and began to write on it with a quill pen, forming the words with many careful flourishes. They reminded Barney of the script on Uncle George's homestead grant. When he had finished that sheet, he got out another and cut a smaller piece from it. Round its edges he inked a heavy black line and then went on writing something else, pausing only once to tell Barney it was time for him to renew the flavour of his gum again. It was all the boy could do to keep his stomach in place the second time he had to put the big slippery cud back in his mouth, but he made himself chew stolidly. Meanwhile, Doc got out a third piece of paper – a huge sheet of thin crackling beautiful parchment – and wrote on that with even more folderols. When he had done, he affixed a huge gold seal to the bottom of it. Adding some red ribbons, he melted a puddle of sealing wax and pressed his big ring into it. Looking up, he smiled in a way that was enough to make Barney hate smiling people for ever.

'An unhappy thought occurred to me. I hope it's an ill-founded suspicion, but it just entered my mind that at some future time you might be tempted to leave the Show without telling me – in other words, to run away. This sort of unruly impulse has a way of creeping in upon the best of us, so to forestall it I've drawn up these papers, which are quite conclusive. Here, read them for yourself.'

He laid them out facing Barney. The first was headed 'Last Will and Testament' and began: 'I, John Morgan, being of sound mind, do hereby make and declare this to be my Last Will and Testament.' After a lot of words that seemed to be mostly 'whereas' and 'hereinbefore' and such meaningless talk, it came down in the last paragraph to state:

And upon my death, I hereby appoint my good friend, Doctor Primus D. Cathcart, to act as guardian to my son, Barney, until such time as my said son shall reach the legal age of twenty-one years.

The second paper was a death certificate for John Morgan dated six months earlier in Mobile, Alabama.

The third, with the fancy scrollwork and the seal, was a document from the Juvenile Court of the Seventy-First District of Alabama, appointing Dr Primus D. Cathcart as legal guardian of Barney Morgan.

'And let me assure you,' said Doc, while he signed each one with different names and in different handwriting, 'that there isn't a sheriff in this Territory who won't be impressed by a gold seal and a bit of red ribbon.'

When he came to the Last Will and Testament, he got out of his drawer the envelope on which Barney had written his note the day before, and while the boy watched in dawning fear he copied the writing of John Morgan as easily as if he were signing his own name.

'You see,' he said lightly, 'if you produce your father's letters and try to claim this is a forgery, the very signature will give you the lie. My boy, you are legally mine, and the sooner you accept the fact and learn to be happy about it, the easier it will be on all of us. If you try to run away, you will be brought back – I can enlist the help of the local law – and then we'll have to work a little harder on convincing you. Of course, I do hope this won't happen. You've got a good spirit, Barney, I'd hate to see you reduced to an abject whimpering little wretch like Billy. I'm afraid, in teaching him, we sacrificed much of his personality. Take your cue from Steve. He seems finally to have accepted his lot – not gracefully, but at least thoroughly and without losing his peculiar glowering character. My dearest wish is that we can all get along together. That's the secret of success in this world, my boy – to get along with people.'

14

BARNEY worked all that afternoon making more 'incense'. Seated on the floor near Doc's desk, he rasped down to dust one stick after another until his arms ached and his fingers were sore from holding on to the rough wood.

Around sundown Maddie brought Doc's dinner to him, but none for Barney.

'You'll sing better on an empty stomach, lad,' explained the medicine man with a smirking kindness that sat more sour on the boy's stomach than had the castor oil.

Of course, Barney had not intended to sing. He'd planned as he sat there that long afternoon on how he would get up on the platform and call out for help, call down to the audience that he was being held a prisoner. And then he thought of the papers in the desk drawer and of how smoothly the doctor could talk, and he knew he didn't have a chance that way. Then he'd decided just to bolt down off the platform and run as hard as he could, up the hill into the mountains, hide out in the darkest hole he could find until they quit hunting for him. But, not having eaten since the day before, he wasn't sure he could run very far. So in the end he tried to rally some of that patience Steve had talked about and even to sing his best that night. If he put on a good show of being 'convinced', maybe he'd be given something to eat and left alone or sent back to Steve for the night. *Just one night*, he promised mentally, *give me just one night and I'll be so far from here. . . .*

*

The audience seemed a little sparse that evening. Their applause sounded thin, and the incense didn't sell very fast. Doc tried to liven things by bringing out a 'Beautifier' which, he told the ladies, was made from rare eucalyptus oil from the Holy Land, but they sat there quiet and watchful and didn't rush up to ask how much it was.

Between the first Show and the second, Hoke came out of the tent looking worried. 'You reckon it's the weather?' he asked Doc in a low voice, glancing up at the murky sky.

'Possibly.' Doc frowned. 'Or possibly the word has spread from that unfortunate incident this morning.'

There were only five or six left in the audience half-way through the second Show and Doc cut the routine short, bid the ladies a flowery good night and gave them each a free pellet of incense to take home.

As soon as the flares were finally put out, Doc ushered the boy back into his wagon, and in a little while Maddie brought a bowl of warmed-over potato chowder. Barney was still tasting castor oil, so he didn't enjoy it much, but it filled his belly and made him feel a little more solid inside. As he ate, the doctor paced up and down the wagon, lost in some thought that was not making him happy. Absently he looked down as the boy finished his meal.

'Yes,' he said, as if talking to himself, 'and we've got to put you somewhere for the night. My own wagon's a trifle crowded just now, but –' His eyes picked at Barney's thoughts. 'How do you feel about Steve? Have you enjoyed taking care of him?'

'I don't mind the chores,' said Barney, scowling a little to hide any piece of eagerness that the doctor might chance to see in his eyes.

'What *do* you mind?'

E

'Well, he's said some mean things about my father. He picks on me – sometimes he makes fun of me.'

Doc rubbed his sharp jaw in that way of his. 'It all may be for your own good in the long run. I believe I'll put you back with him again – at least temporarily.'

Elated with the success of his own first try at play-acting, Barney carried it a step farther. He hung back and dragged his feet as they made the short walk to the strong man's wagon, and actually had to be urged up the stairs and herded in at the door.

Steve was washing the oil off himself as they came in. He turned his head slightly, but didn't seem much interested as Doc said, 'I've brought the boy back to you, Steve. I'd advise you to have a talk with him – see if you can persuade him of the futility of walking off the job again. And so that you won't lose him before he's had a chance to become convinced, I believe we'll lock your door tonight.'

Barney's heart sank at that, but Steve only shrugged as if it made no difference.

It was a bad sound – that padlock clicking shut outside. Barney drew in a deep shivery breath to speak, but Steve held up a hand quickly to stop him.

In a gruff tone the strong man said, fairly loudly, 'Well, now that you're back, suppose you make up for lost time. Go straighten my bed and then pour me some fresh water.'

Barney did as he was told, realizing that this was part of the fierce game they were playing and that the strong man knew how to do it better than he did. Steve went over and set his ear against the door, held it there for several minutes. Finally he straightened up.

'There he goes,' he said softly. 'I knew he'd hang around and listen a while.' He groped his way over to Barney's side, and for a minute they stood awkwardly silent. Then he put out a hand and found the boy's shoulder, took a hard grip on it. 'I'm sorry you got caught. Come on, tell me what happened.'

Together they sat down on the bunk. Speaking in whispers, Barney told everything from start to finish. The strong man listened without too much surprise, nodding once in a while, laughing silently when he heard about the castor oil. And when the story was finally finished, Steve sat back, thoughtful.

'So now you know most of it,' he said.

'But why didn't you tell me? Why didn't you come right out in the beginning and tell me what was going on?'

'Would you have believed me? After what Doc told you about my being addled?'

'You knew he told me that!'

'Oh, yes,' said Steve with an odd smile. 'I knew it. It's better anyway that you found out for yourself. There's no substitute for experience. Question is, now that your eyes are open, what are you going to do?'

'Run away,' answered Barney promptly. 'Run so far away his papers won't do him any good.'

Slowly Steve nodded. 'I'll help you.'

'Will you come with me?'

For a minute the blind face lit up almost as if its eyes had been given vision, and then Steve slumped back into the same old position, elbows on his knees, head bent.

'I'll admit I'd thought of it,' he said. 'In fact, I didn't think of much else for a while. But today, after you left, I did some more thinking. You see, I thought you were gone for good, and I was glad – for your sake. I'd only hold you back, Barney. You could make it alone, but the two of us might not. And Doc would follow me harder and farther than he would you. I'm the backbone of his Show.' He shook his head. 'No, it's best that you go by yourself.'

Barney had thought of this already – that a blind man would be slow company on the road. But now that he heard Steve say it himself, it called up all his stubbornness. A new feeling had begun to come over him where Steve was concerned, something he'd never known before. It wasn't the same thing he felt for his father, and certainly not the silly worshipful wonder he'd felt for Doc. This was an equal feeling – he supposed it was what people really meant when they said the word 'friend'.

'I won't go without you!' he said, sounding a little pompous and stiff with his own shyness. 'Maybe you are blind, but I'm almighty small. I reckon we need each other.'

The strong man frowned and put his hands up to hold his head, as if the problem were too heavy to figure.

'You know what I think?' said Barney in a rush. 'I think you think too much!'

It made Steve look up. His face straightened out of its frown and got firm. He held out his hand to Barney in a man-sized clasp.

'All right,' he said, 'we'll do it.'

The kind of fight a carnival man
knows best – a free-for-all between
Show people and 'townies'

15

'IF we try to skip out on the Show here in town,' Steve mused, 'we'll be easy to track. It would be better if we could slip away while they're on the move somewhere so that they wouldn't know where to start looking for us.'

'I can wait,' asserted Barney staunchly.

'Can you? Can you take their orders day after day and act just rebellious enough so that they don't get suspicious and yet not enough to get put under stricter "training"? There's no telling how long Doc will choose to stay here, but as long as we're marking time he'll be watching us like a hawk. One false move, and he'll separate us so fast –! He's still not sure of me, you know. I've tried to get away twice now, and though he threatened some fairly grim things if I were to try it again, he's not sure I won't,' Steve chuckled. 'He's dead right too.' There was a new air of lightness and excitement about him, just in these few minutes since Barney had talked him into escaping. 'Fact is, I'm not sure that I can wait myself. I wish we could try it tonight, but the hole's not big enough yet.'

'What hole?'

'Here, beneath the bunk. Take a look.'

Barney got down on the floor and squirmed under the low-slung bed. In the middle, close to the wall of the wagon, he found a good-sized opening whittled out of the wood of the bottom, clear through to where he could dimly see the ground and get a draught of night air from outside. Remembering the miner's big Bowie knife which Steve had taken charge of, he knew how it had been done, and it seemed such a good joke he felt like laughing.

Scrambling back out, he said, 'It's good, Steve. It's almost big enough for me. If I could just get out –' Barney was thinking aloud now. 'I'll bet . . . I'll bet I could fix it so we'd move on.'

'How?' Steve wanted to know.

Thoughtfully he listened to Barney's idea; after he'd considered it a minute, he nodded.

'It's chancy, but it might work if you're quiet enough. Here, let's see if I can't whittle away enough wood to get you out.' Reaching under the bedding, Steve got out the big gleaming knife. Then he wormed his way under the bunk, and Barney heard the small sound of a blade digging into wood.

While the strong man worked on the hole, Barney took a cup, opened the door of the stove – thanking his stars that there had been no time to build a fire in it tonight – and reached up into the stove-pipe to scrape loose some of the heavy black soot. When he'd collected half a cupful, he straightened up, put out the lantern so that the window would show dark, and waited.

The rest of the camp quietened down as the others went to bed, and the night got later and later. Still Steve worked on. The bite of each cut began to sound loud to Barney, and sometimes he found himself holding his breath, listening for a footstep outside or any sound that might mean trouble. It seemed like a long time before the strong man finally shoved himself out from under the bunk, stretching silently to relieve his cramped limbs.

Softly he said, 'Go on, see if it's big enough yet.'

Keeping his cup of stoveblack handy, Barney crawled under and found the hole. As he felt around the cut, he thought he could make it, though he hated to imagine what would happen if he got stuck half-way. There was no choice but to go out head-first, so shrinking his shoulders together, he wriggled down into the hole, squirmed and twisted and came down with a dull thump on to the soft ground under the wagon.

For a minute he lay still, listening to the slam-bang of his own heart. There wasn't any other sound in the close quiet of the night, so he moved at last, reached up into the hole and felt for the cup of soot. As he found it, he heard Steve's whisper: 'Be careful!'

With the sky still overcast, there wasn't so much as the light of a few stars to help him. The darkness was a thick soft black blanket in front of his face, something so near he wanted to brush it away with his hand. Moving only a step at a time, he groped his way round the tent, barking his shins on guy ropes, feeling his way round the tent stakes. It occurred to him that this was what Steve was up against all the time, and he wondered suddenly how the strong man had contrived to run away before.

He'd reached Doc's wagon now and stood outside listening, every inch of him on pins for the least stir inside. But the window in front was dark and all was still. After a few minutes he tiptoed up the steps, dipped his fingers in the soot and drew them noiselessly across the bare panel of the door, hoping hard that the black was leaving a good thick mark. Made a 3. Then a 7. Got some more soot for the 77. Still not a sound from inside.

Next, to Hoke's wagon. Barney got the first number written on the door – and, inside, the poodle barked! At the sound he jumped and froze, didn't move until he heard Maddie say sleepily, 'Suzette, be quiet!' That unfixed him. Quickly he smeared a seven and two more sevens, which caused Suzette to set up a whole racket inside and made Hoke speak out in a grouchy voice.

'Fer the love of mud, let the pup out.'

Barney slipped down off the steps and got out of there. Skipping and skidding round the tent, stubbing his toes over a half-dozen obstacles, he reached his own wagon. Just as he was about to duck under again, he remembered that it wouldn't be a good thing if his door were the only one without any numbers. Hastily he ran round to the back and made the symbol on the panels, while on the far side of the tent a big commotion was being set up. Somebody had lit a lantern – streamers of light pitched and tossed, and Maddie's voice rose shriller than Suzette's barking as she called to Hoke.

'Come out here! Look at this!'

As Barney scuttled under the wagon, he saw the light go on in Doc's window too. And now, in his haste, he couldn't get back up through the hole. Try every way he could, he couldn't fit his shoulders in right. Steve tried to help him back inside, but it wouldn't work. About then Suzette came tearing around the tent, her nose to the ground, following the exact path of his footsteps. When she discovered Barney under the wagon, she flung herself on him happily, trying to lick his face.

'Get away – get away!' He shoved her back, but she wouldn't be put off, and he determined furiously that there had never been such a stupid dog.

He could see lights moving and heard them following her now. Crawling out on the far side of the wagon, he hesitated, for there was nowhere to run except across the open clearing, which would make him easy enough to spot.

As he was about to chance it and run anyhow, he felt a timid touch from above – a hand had reached down from the wagon box to pluck at his collar. He looked up in time to catch just a gleam of the whites of Billy's scared eyes. Losing no time, Barney hoisted himself up into the box and huddled down under the blanket with the coloured boy, who was shaking so hard his tremors threatened to shiver the whole wagon.

Doc and Hoke had reached the spot now. 'Go to it, Suzie,' the fat man was puffing. 'Find 'im, find 'im.'

As the silly thing ran round and round the wagon in circles, Doc said, with some annoyance, 'I never saw her act that way before. She usually follows track like a beeline. Unless. . . .' He came to stand under the driver's box. 'Billy?'

The coloured boy shuddered, then unwillingly stuck his head out from under the blanket. 'Yes, suh?' he quavered.

'You hear anything strange going on around here just now?'

'Yes, suh, lots of hoo-raw.'

'I don't mean that! Did you hear anyone fooling around the wagons?'

'No, suh, I keep my head under this here blanket, I do.'

'Well, now that it's out from under the blanket,' said Doc impatiently, 'take a look on top of the wagon and make sure there's nobody hiding there.'

Billy took a hasty peep. 'No, suh, ain't nobody up there.'

Now, from the sound of his voice, Barney judged the doctor was walking away, saying to Hoke, 'I guess the fellow's given us the slip. Confound it, I'd like to have caught him. This may be some prank, but then again . . .'

'You thinkin' what I'm thinkin'?' asked Hoke glumly. 'What all these folks been tellin' about Vigilantes and such?'

'I'm thinking', said Doc, 'that we'd better get out. It's too bad – there's a good deal more money to be made here. But I suppose that business in town today must have spread fast. So – let us get dressed. Steve!' He paused and knocked at the door of the wagon. 'Get dressed and ready to help break camp.'

Barney got set to move fast now, but still he took time to whisper his thanks to Billy.

'Don't say it, Mist' Barney,' moaned the coloured boy. 'I ain't seen you here t'night. I ain't seen *nobody!*' And he began to draw on his boots.

When Barney got back under the wagon, he found Steve hacking feverishly at the hole to make it a little bigger, and this time he managed to scrounge his way through.

For a minute the two of them lay on the floor of the wagon, panting. Then Steve nudged him.

'Don't ever complain to me again about being skinny,' he said. 'If you had a little more weight, we wouldn't have made it!'

16

IT was on the long trip down the Gulch that night that Steve told Barney his story.

The wagon rocked and bumped too much for them to try to sleep; it was all they could do to keep from being thrown around against the fixtures, which were all nailed in place and full of fairly sharp corners. Barney did a good deal of grumbling at first, ranting against Doc for being so inhuman as to keep them locked up inside a swaying jolting old box of a wagon. But he finally noticed that Steve wasn't joining in, so he quietened down and let the strong man show him how to sit on the floor and brace his feet to hold firm against the worst of the bumps.

'It won't be so bad when we get on the level,' Steve added. 'After all, this is what we wanted – to get going. Tomorrow I'll try to make some more headway on that hole, and two or three days from now we'll be out of here.'

So, feeling a little ashamed of his outburst, Barney settled down to the tedious ride. After a while he said, 'Tell me about the other times you tried to get away.'

Speaking slowly, in a voice that was almost dry of emotion, Steve began to tell of his younger life. He'd gone blind after a sickness, so early he could hardly remember what it was like to see. He told how his father had thought of him as a burden and treated him like one of the livestock. He'd been put to work on heavy lifting and pulling jobs, because he always had been good and husky. By the time he was about twelve he had enough muscle so that Doc, when he came along, saw profit in it.

'He'd paid my father fifty dollars,' Steve said, 'and promised to treat me like his own son. I was glad enough to go with him. I was billed as the "Boy Wonder" in those days – my act was to lift one end of a wagon. It wasn't as heavy as it probably looked, but it must have impressed the crowd. After the Show Doc used to take up a collection, saying the money was to get my eyes doctored. I believed him. I even admired him then.'

Barney was silently relieved to hear Steve confess it. He'd been thinking himself ten ways a gullible fool to have ever believed Doc about anything.

'Then one night,' Steve went on, 'a real doctor happened to be in the crowd, and right in the middle of Doc's pitch he offered to come up and give me a free examination. He asked me a few questions and looked at my eyes through some instrument he had, and right there on Doc's own stage he announced that I couldn't ever be cured and that Doc was a fake. The shock of finding out the truth did something to me. I got to thinking about the right and wrong of things, and the next town we hit, when Doc started to take up his collection, something got into me. I couldn't just stand by – I shouted out the truth to the crowd. So that made two towns in a row we had to leave in a hurry, and that's when my "training" began.' There was a hard note of irony in the way he said it.

'If I wanted to eat, I had to go through my act, but Doc didn't try to take up any more collections. Instead, he began to try to build my muscles, put me through exercises for hours, but he didn't know much about it, and I just got tired without getting much stronger. About that time they got Billy – he wasn't more than ten or so then, and Doc put him to work leading me around, doing the chores. It wasn't long before we began to plot to get away.'

'Was Billy different in those days?' Barney asked curiously.

'Bill was as sparky as a cricket,' Steve said. 'He used to dance – some sort of barefoot jig that they call "skiffling" down south. That was his part in the bally before he learned to juggle. He was full of mettle and sore from being nipped by Hoke's whip. So one night we took off, thinking we'd get away from Doc for good and find some way to make our living – there ought to be some sort of work for a man as strong as I am. Of course we didn't make it. Some farmer's dogs came down on us, and the farmer held us until morning, when Doc came hunting us with the sheriff. He showed papers stating he was my guardian. I began to realize what valuable property I was.' Steve laughed curtly.

'What did he do to you for running away?' Barney asked, shivering.

'Separated us, of course. He gave Billy over to Hoke to be "convinced", and Doc himself put me through a couple of bad days – he's got more tricks than just chewing gum. After that he took me into some town and hired a professional weight-lifter to build me up into the strongest man in the world. That's when I met Ojo.'

'That was his name?'

Steve nodded, and his voice took on a sadness Barney had never heard in it before. 'He was a foreigner, a wrestler; he taught me the exercises, the control, and the knack. But Ojo taught me more than just how to use my body. I was with him all day, every day. He taught me to speak – he admired the English language, even though it wasn't his own – and he taught me to listen, which is more important. Besides that, he was a good friend. After a few months with him I hated Doc more than ever. I guess it showed, too, because that's when Ojo got sent away.' He shook his head angrily and fell silent.

Barney finally asked, 'Why was he sent away? Where?'

The strong man said slowly, 'Somebody wrote a letter to the authorities and said Ojo wasn't a good citizen. It wasn't true – he loved this country more than most of its natives do. But people are suspicious of anybody different from themselves, so they sent him away. Very handy, from Doc's point of view. It so happened he hadn't paid for my instruction yet.'

'You think Doc wrote the letter with the lies in it!'

'I'm sure of it.'

'You and me and everybody!' cried Barney furiously. 'Doc's cheated us all!'

'That's what I got to thinking. When we got back to the Show and I discovered they'd turned Billy into a shivering little coward, I got mad and surly and wouldn't do my act. But Doc was ready for that. He'd made out a paper saying I was mentally unbalanced and dangerously violent, and he had me put in a crazy house – strapped down to a bed in a room full of gibbering idiots until I gave up and promised to go through with the Samson stunt. That business in the asylum shook me up to where I stayed in line for a long time – I couldn't see how I could win. And then, not so long ago, we started north and something happened that got me hopeful again.'

'You mean when I came with the Show?'

'No, just before that. We were coming through Utah, near some city named Salt Lake, I think, and Doc tried to set up the tent. Well, he was told to move on fast. Those folks don't hold with medicine fakers. So as we came north and I heard people talk hostile to him, I got the idea that maybe, if I could get away to them, they'd listen to me instead of Doc when he came looking for me. The night I decided to try it, I gave Billy one more chance to get away – I think if he'd come along, we would have made it. I even threatened to break his neck, but it didn't help. He just sat glued to the seat and kept on driving, so I slipped off without him.'

'Alone!' Barney said, shocked. 'You could never make it alone.'

'No, I guess not. The minute they found out I was gone, they unhitched one of the teams and rode back. That blasted little poodle has been trained to track, and she found where I'd turned off the road. So when I heard them coming, I played it the only way I could – I pretended to be glad to be found. I made out that it was all a big mistake. Doc chose to act as if he believed me, but he wasn't fooled much. He didn't lose any time putting that padlock on the door.'

'It was lucky they put me in with you,' said Barney.

'Doc had misgivings about it,' Steve assured him, 'but none of them wanted to be bothered taking care of me, and Billy couldn't be wheedled or forced into this wagon, even at the end of Hoke's whip. So when Doc told me he was bringing you here, he threatened me against turning you "bitter" with my own "prejudices" – which meant I was not to warn you about him and the Show. He said he had big plans for you and that he'd fixed it so you wouldn't believe anything I'd say anyhow, by telling you I was crazy. Of course, I was sure that it wouldn't be long before an alert kid like you would figure things out for yourself, so there was nothing to do but wait and try to keep relations between us from sounding so friendly that Doc would be suspicious.'

And that completed the story. Barney was silent a while, and then he laughed. 'Well, even if we get caught,' he said, 'there's one thing Doc can't do. There aren't any crazy houses around here.'

Steve didn't answer that at once. Finally he said, 'No, and I guess he knows it, too. At least, he's thought up a new bluff – if it is a bluff.'

'You mean he threatened you with something else?'

Slowly the strong man said, 'I don't know how much of a doctor he really is – I guess he's had some sort of medical training. Enough, he says, to perform an operation that would fix me so I could never speak again. He said if I enlisted your help, it would be the last time I'd ever ask for assistance.'

17

THEY travelled four days straight, stopping only to rest the horses and let everybody catch a short sleep now and then. Barney was let out long enough to help with the chores, but he moved in a thick atmosphere of unsociability. Sore and disgusted from being cooped up inside the jolting wagon, he didn't find it hard to put on a dark look, and as for the others, they offered him no more words than to tell him curtly what to do. It was plain they all blamed him for their recent flight, and none of them made the least attempt to pretend any pleasantness.

At times when they were halted, even Steve resumed the gloomy air of half-mockery, half-impatience – did it so well that Barney smarted under some of his remarks and had to remind himself that it was just pretence. But the minute the teams were hitched and the two of them locked up together, the strong man would soften his voice and they'd go to planning again.

Their route was down the big valley along the bank of the Jefferson River, which was, as Barney told Steve, a fair-sized torrent by then, made up out of the joining of the Beaverhead, the Ruby, and the Big Hale rivers. It was taking them almost due north, and that was fine with Barney. He wasn't sure where Pipestone Pass was, exactly, but he figured it must be in the range of mountains that showed like a ragged dark blue rampart on the north-west horizon, coming closer each day.

The hole in the floor was coming fairly well, though it was

going to need more work before Steve could get his massive shoulders through it. There were times when the going along the rutted old stage road was too rough for him to make any headway. At times like those, all they could do was to sit braced and talk.

Barney wondered what they'd do if they couldn't find his father in Butte; he suggested they might pan some gold of their own. He tried to explain how it was done, though he wasn't too sure about it in his own mind.

At one point Steve said, 'Well, just what *is* gold?'

Barney remembered the nugget old Skinner had given him and got it out. Steve rolled it between his fingers and asked what it looked like.

'Not much,' admitted Barney. 'It's a sort of dirty yellow.'

'And why does this stuff drive men so?'

'Well, it buys things,' Barney told him. 'That nugget would buy us food for a couple of months.'

Steve shook his head. 'Not if you came among people who'd rather keep their food than take gold for it. Oh, I know, Barney – I know there has to be some means of paying for your needs. But I can't help wondering what there is in this –' he handed back the nugget – 'cold and hard as it is, to make men go lawless and steal or kill or die for it.'

Barney wondered silently how they always got into these questions that he couldn't answer. On the other hand, there were times when he expected an argument and didn't get it.

Ever since the night Billy had saved his neck, it had been on Barney's conscience at least to give him a chance to make the break with them, but in view of Steve's stern attitude he had hesitated to bring the subject up. On the fourth day out, though, he decided it had to be talked over, and launched into his reasons earnestly.

'Billy's been decent to me,' he said. 'He warned me, way back the second day I was with the Show – told me not to stay here. He tried to help me with the juggling, and I'd sure enough been a goner that night if he hadn't let me up on the box with him. I think we ought to give him another chance.'

The strong man listened and shrugged. 'If you feel you have to do a thing in order to keep square with yourself, don't ever ask anybody's advice. It's your own business.' And that was that.

When they made camp that evening, Barney watched for an opening to talk to the coloured boy. He found his chance when they took the horses down to water them. Standing on the bank of the river in the last glow of warm lazy afternoon sunlight with the first cool night air beginning to stir, Barney was usually glad enough just to be still and watch the horses' ears work back and forth as they drank. It was about the only quiet time he had these days. The green country spread out broad around them, and the only sound at that time of day was the hushed chuckling of the water as it boiled and broke over the rocks.

That evening, under cover of the river's noise, he spoke to Billy, who stood only a few feet away.

'We're going to try it one of these days,' he said softly. He didn't turn or even look in the coloured boy's direction, but kept his eyes fixed on the big gentle heads of the horses lowered to the water at his feet. 'If you want to come – ? Billy – do you hear what I say?'

Billy let out a long shaky whisper of words. 'Don't tell me, I don't wanta know!'

'I am telling you. You've been nice to me, and you hate these people, too. You could come with us and maybe get a job somewhere. I'll bet folks will pay to see good juggling. And Steve said you used to dance –'

Billy shook himself all over, a little like a dog shivers off the rain. 'Man can't dance when he's scared and I'm scared! Don't ask me, Mist' Barney.'

'What are you scared of?'

'You don't know how 'tis when they catch you.'

'They're not going to catch us. We're going to fool them this time. We're going –'

'Don't tell me,' pleaded the coloured boy mournfully. 'I hope you do it, but it ain't easy. Ain't easy at all.'

'Maybe you don't want to risk it with Steve again, seeing that he's kind of slow-moving. That's all right. Don't come with us. Stay here and let them think they can trust you, and wait your chance. Then, next time they get near a town, duck out by yourself and hide somewhere for a while. They'll get tired of looking and go on, and then you can come out of hiding and go in town and get a job. And while you're looking, take this.' Barney dug down into the pocket of his denims. He hadn't really thought it out carefully – the nugget was really his father's, of course, but he knew how John Morgan would feel about honouring a debt. 'Here.' He flipped it across, and Billy caught it automatically, looked at it almost frightened.

'That's gold!' He tested the nugget in his teeth tentatively, rubbed it on his sleeve. 'That's gold, all right. I seen some back in town, gentleman paid for his Curative with a chunk of that.' He looked straight across at Barney, and deep in the sad dark eyes there was a kind of wonder. 'That's the first spendin' stuff I ever did have!'

He glanced over his shoulder quickly, saw that no one was watching them, and shoved the nugget deep in his pocket. Then, grabbing up the lead ropes of the horses, he led them up the bank in a hurry. He was half-way back to the wagons before Barney got his own team turned round. And as they went about staking out the horses, Barney thought he could see a difference in the way Billy held himself.

He was so busy thinking about that, he jumped almost out of his shoes when he heard his name called sharply from behind him.

Doc and Hoke stood together in the middle of the semicircle of wagons, and as he came up, they both scowled.

'Not a sign of a town these past four days,' Doc told him accusingly. 'No settlement bigger than a stage station. We left a lucrative prosperous community because of you, my lad, and now you had better direct us to where the nearest gold camp is. I'd intended to make inquiry in Virginia City, but our hasty departure didn't permit that. Just below here there is a ford across the river. A track of sorts leads off towards the mountains west of here. Do they contain gold and gold-miners? The main road follows the river east. What lies there? Speak up, now!'

Barney hesitated. A swift thought crossed his mind that Doc would be suspicious if he were too eager to head for the mountains, so, putting on a pout, he said, 'I don't know about any other gold camps.'

Without warning, Hoke's hand moved. The flat back of it caught Barney a bruising blow across the mouth, knocking him sideways into the grass on his knees.

In a dangerously quiet voice Doc said, 'Now tell us what you know of this country.'

Getting up slowly, Barney licked his lips where they still stung. Speaking reluctantly, he said, 'Well, I've heard about one town north of here. If you follow this river far enough, you get to a place called Helena, and I think there's gold there.'

He glanced off towards the mountains and said even more slowly, 'I heard there were silver mines on the other side of those mountains.'

'I've heard of this here Helena,' Hoke said. 'I heard it's rich. I vote we head that way. Easy travellin' by the river. Plenty of water.'

Doc began to pace back and forth. 'I wonder what sort of community it is.'

Barney ventured another word. 'It's the capital of the Territory, where the government is. I think it's pretty much like Virginia City – at least, there's a telegraph line between them.'

The doctor eyed him. 'You turned out to be fairly well versed in Montana geography after all.'

Barney didn't explain that the only reason he knew about it was because Uncle George had lived there once for a while and was always talking about it.

Hoke was scowling. 'Telegraph line I don't specially care fer. You reckon it's true?'

'Probably,' Doc told him dryly. 'Barney made the acquaintance of some Western Union men on that eventful trip of his to town. Well, my boy, it will suit me far better to go to some community which cannot have been forewarned of our coming.' He smiled contemptuously. 'Tomorrow we head for the mountains.'

18

BARNEY stood on tiptoe at the window in the front of the wagon and peered out past the driver's box, trying to see through the deepening dusk. Close beside him, Steve waited, quiet and ready as a cocked gun. The going was bumpy, but they hung on and stood, and after a minute Barney said in a low voice, 'There's no sign of any place to pull off – the road's narrow and the mountains go up steep on either side. It's almost dark down here, but the sky is still a little light.'

'We'd better wait until it's good and dark.'

'I don't know,' Barney told him dubiously. 'The moon is over half full and it's rising early these nights.'

Steve swore softly. 'The moon! I forget things like that.' Then he said, 'You'll have to decide when the time is right.'

'I'd say pretty soon. The longer we're gone before they find a place to camp, the farther away we'll be from here.'

In the dimness the strong man nodded. 'I'll go first. Then if anybody happens to look back and see me, you stay put and pretend you were asleep. No point in our both getting blamed.'

'I don't think they'll see us. The road is pretty twisty here and they'll be watching for chuck holes.'

Silently they got ready. Each stowed away a small packet of food scraps, bits of bread and meat that they'd managed to save from their meals the past three days as they awaited their chance to escape, while all the time the teams had hauled the big wagons higher and higher up the Pass into the heart of the mountains. Steve stuck the knife in his belt, and Barney put on his Mackinaw. Excitement was beginning to pound inside him.

In the heavy gloom of the wagon he saw Steve crawl under the bunk, saw the long legs work gradually out of sight, and then they were gone. If there'd been any noise, it had been covered up by the racking clatter and creak of the old wagon.

Trembling inwardly, Barney scrambled under the bunk. The hole was so much bigger he almost fell through before he was ready. There was a brief frightening few seconds when his head hung down right beside the grinding churning big wheel. Then he touched the rocky ground moving beneath him – let go and came down on it. He skinned his knees a little, but the sting was lost in the sudden elation of success as he saw the wagon go trundling off up the Pass, leaving him crouched motionless in the roadway. It seemed like hours, rather than minutes, before the wagon got swallowed up in the gathering darkness.

At last he dared move. Turning his head, he made out the shadow that was Steve, lying still as himself, just as they had agreed, waiting until they were well clear of the wagons. Now he got up and went cautiously back to the strong man's side.

'They're gone,' he whispered, helping Steve up.

'Can we get off the road here?'

'Too steep.'

'Then we'll backtrack until you can spot a break in the hills.' The strong man held on to his shoulder, and Barney led the way quickly through the dusk until he found a place where the road crossed a dry ravine. He hesitated, peering up it.

'It's pretty steep – hard to tell where it goes,' he told Steve.

'Anything's better than staying on the road. At least they can't follow us on horseback. Let's try it.'

As they began to climb, it went better than Barney had expected, especially with the strong man to boost him over the worst places. Steve was fairly good at climbing, feeling his way up over the rocks almost like an animal, by instinct. It was when they hit the occasional open spots where they could walk that he grew uncertain and stumbled a lot. They moved without speaking, their senses keyed backwards for sounds of pursuit. When the first little yap broke the stillness far behind them, they both heard it and stiffened.

'Was that –?' whispered Barney.

Steve didn't answer until it came again, the high-pitched barking of a dog.

'It's Suzette,' he said tightly. 'They must have stopped soon after we left and discovered we were gone.' Barney heard the dead-flat discouragement in his voice, and his own heart sank as he realized what it meant.

'Come on!' urged the boy. 'We've got to hurry!'

A hundred feet farther on, they reached an open spot where the walls of the ravine drew apart, and Barney realized with a shock that the moon was already up and bright. It flooded the grassy glade, and what he saw ruined one of his hopes. He'd been thinking they had better get out of this gully, but now he saw the shelving walls where old flash floods had worn the earth away to bare rimrock, too sheer to climb. There was nothing to do but keep on up the ravine.

They were running now as fast as they could with Steve stumbling and tripping every other step. The poodle's yap followed them, sometimes seeming far behind, sometimes sounding much nearer, but always there, coming on.

Once the strong man fell. As he got to his feet, he just stood, a hulking dark figure under the moonlight, and shook his head. 'Go on without me, Barney.'

'I won't!' The boy caught his arm and hurried him along. Up ahead, the banks of the ravine narrowed again sharply and the way was plunged in darkness. If they could just get out of the white flood of moonlight, Barney thought, they'd be safer. It wasn't until they'd reached the shadows that his hopes gave out. A big slide had come down off the heights in some long-past time and blocked the ravine, once and for all. At the very bottom of the pile was a boulder as big as a house.

Barney stopped below it, gasping for breath.

'What is it? Are you winded?' demanded Steve.

'N-no. . . .' The boy couldn't help it – his voice was shaking in spite of him. 'I stopped because we can't go on. I brought us up a box canyon, Steve. We're up against a solid rock wall!'

The strong man reached out and put his hands against it. 'How high?'

'Too high. Thirty feet, maybe.'

'Is there a foothold anywhere on it?'

Barney peered up through the dark and made out a scrub pine that had somehow taken root in the rock face about half-way up. 'If we could reach that, I think we could climb the rest of the way. But we can't, so –'

'Could you reach it by standing on my shoulders?'

'I'm not sure.'

Without wasting any more time, the strong man picked the boy up and Barney found himself astraddle the broad shoulders. Setting himself close to the rock, Steve said, 'Get up on your feet, easy – that's it.'

But Barney's fingers, stretching as far as he could reach, were still a foot short of the gnarly little tree. He was about to give up when he felt the strong man take hold of his ankles with hands like steel clamps and begin to lift him higher.

Feeling his way up over the rough rock, Barney finally laid hold of the tree and with a desperate heave got himself belly-across it.

'We did it!' he breathed, with a surge of relief. And then it ebbed away again, leaving him empty and frightened. Because as soon as he looked down, he realized that there was no way for Steve to follow. In fact, the strong man had stepped back a few paces, his hands hanging at his sides in quiet acceptance.

'Steve –!'

'Listen to me, Barney,' he interrupted quickly, but without much agitation. 'There isn't time to argue. You're going to be on your own now, so you can't afford to panic and you can't think too much about me. Just figure it was a good try and I'm no worse off than I was before – No! Don't talk! Listen to me. I can't tell you how to find your way out of these mountains and down to where there are people, but you've got five good senses and a level head. If you start getting excited, sit down and close your eyes. Figure your way out. Don't run headlong. Now go on and climb up the rest of the way, and don't wait to see what happens to me. You can't help me any more except to save yourself. If you do that, it will give me one good thing to think about.'

'Steve!'

'Good-bye.' Firmly the strong man cut off his cry of distress and turned to walk back down into the moonlight of the glade. Feeling his way, he found a grassy flat spot, then stood and waited.

The clamour of the little dog was close by now, and it wasn't a minute later that Barney, rooted helpless on his perch, saw Doc and Hoke come out of the shadows below. They'd been hurrying, but as they saw they had their quarry at bay, they slowed down and grew cautious. Steve had the big Bowie knife out, holding it in his hand, and as Barney saw the glint of moonlight off the blade, he had a brief moment of hope.

Hoke had ordered the poodle to heel, and now he shook the kinks out of the blacksnake whip that he carried, flipping it out to its full length.

Doc held up a hand to check him; he spoke out, and in the night stillness, Barney could hear every word.

'Are you going to pretend to be glad we've found you this time, Steve?'

The strong man shook his head. 'No. No more games.'

'Where's the boy?'

'Where you can't follow him.'

'It's of small matter. He was becoming a disturbing factor to the whole troupe. I could have trained him in time, but I'm actually just as glad we're rid of him. He won't survive long in this wilderness. You, though, are another matter. Do you intend to be difficult?'

'Just as difficult as possible.' Steve sounded grim and determined.

'You haven't a chance, you know. You'd better make your peace with us. Or don't you recall what I warned you would happen?' he continued with a sneer.

'I remember practically everything you've ever said to me,' the strong man said, clear and defiant. 'There wasn't much worth in any of it, either. I'll tell you how much peace you'll get from me – you may be able to take me, but you'll never make me perform for you again. I'd not lift so much as my finger to help you get rich off sucker money. I'd rather starve right here –'

'Oh, no, Steve,' Doc said with deadly pleasantry, at the same time taking down a length of rope that he had looped over his shoulder. 'You're too valuable to meet such an end.'

He started towards the strong man, who, alerted by the sound, set himself to fight, the knife half raised. With a sudden hiss and a snap, the whip snaked out and wrapped itself round his wrist. Steve held on to his weapon, but in trying to shake loose, he lost valuable time and Doc was circling in behind him, the noose of rope ready in his hands. Steve half turned to meet him, but Hoke drew back his arm and the whip lashed out again, this time catching the strong man about the ankles. At the exact instant it wrapped tight, Hoke heaved back on it and Steve went down. Before he could scramble up, Doc moved in with cat-like quickness. A well-aimed kick sent the knife flying, the rope pinned the strong man's arms, and now Hoke leaped in to help. For a minute the three of them thrashed about together in a terrible silent combat. Then, abruptly, the glade grew still.

Slowly Doc stood up, breathing hard, and dusted his hands. Hoke straightened, too, nursing one knee.

'He kicked me, the dirty –' For a minute he stood and abused the man who lay bound and helpless on the ground. Angrily he turned to Doc and pleaded. 'This time he's got it comin'. Let me take some skin off him!'

'That's for the youngsters, Hoke,' Doc told him impatiently. 'Put your toy away. He'll get his reward for this night's annoyance in due time. Right now, suppose we get him back to camp.'

They hauled the strong man to his feet, and he made no further resistance. It was as if the constriction of the ropes on his arms had cut off his will to fight.

A dry hard hurt knotted up inside Barney as he watched them lead the powerful trussed figure down the ravine. Long after the sounds of their going had dwindled off far below and quiet settled in, the boy clung to his perch, rigid with anguish.

He wanted to cry, but tears wouldn't come. He tried to think of his own risky future – he even tried to be afraid for himself – but it didn't amount to a drop beside the whole tide of fear that swam over him when he thought of what was going to happen to Steve.

19

WHEN Barney woke next morning, it was to know the same despair of the night before. He wondered dully how he'd managed to sleep at all, bunched down under a shelf of rock with the Mackinaw loose over him like a small tent – all that stood between him and the night animals that lived in the mountains. Even in his half-sleep he'd been dimly aware of little runnings and cryings and movements around him, and now, as he crept out into the early sunlight, he knew he'd not got much rest.

He ate some of the bread he'd brought along and tried to think what to do. He couldn't get beyond one impulse to go back to the road through the Pass and try to keep in touch with the wagons, though how that was going to help Steve he didn't know.

Since they might be watching for him near the foot of the ravine, he decided to play it cautious and take a cut-off over the hills. There must be another ravine he could follow down to the Pass farther up ahead, where they wouldn't be expecting him. He'd hide and wait for them, and then – well, he'd figure that out when he came to it.

Guessing at his direction as well as he could, he started off through the thick forest, but soon found himself in a bewildering maze of hills creased deep with dry washes and gullies. None of them had any water in them, and he was thirsty – his throat was swelling with dryness. To stave off his growing anxiety, he ate the last of his meagre provisions and started along a new ridge. But as the sun hung straight overhead in the sky, he wasn't sure which way he was going. The ground rose steeper until finally, looking up through the trees, he caught a glimpse of a towering rimrock cliff far above. The sight of it sent a cold weakness over him.

Rushing back the way he had come, he plunged across the mountain meadows covered with new-sprung flowers; there was mockery in the mild beautiful warmth of the day. Heart pumping, he began to run with a sort of nameless fear, ploughing through tangled deadwood, leaping from boulder to boulder. And then, in his headlong flight, he tripped over a fallen log and sprawled hard on his face in the pine needles. It knocked the wind out of him and somehow jarred some of the sense back.

As he lay there, gasping for breath, he thought of Steve. *Don't run. Sit down and figure.* Painfully the boy picked himself up and sank down on to a log.

'I'm lost,' he said out loud. Then, bluffly, he said, 'I'm *good* and lost. And thirsty, too.'

Close your eyes. So he did. Tried to think where he could go to find water. Snow piles up deepest on the northern face of a hill – it stays there longest, and the best drainage is always on a north slope. Opening his eyes, he looked around. The sun was far enough down in the sky so that he could locate himself; he was on a south slope. Getting to his feet, making himself move slowly, he headed into the sun, watching all the while for a shift in the hills. It wasn't long until he saw a saddle stretching across to a new system of ridges. Following it, he found himself on a north face. Half an hour later he came to a freshet – it wasn't much more than a trickle of melt, but it made good drinking.

Lying beside it, he filled up, a little bit at a time, until he couldn't hold any more. It would have been a good thing, he thought, just to stay right here, but he didn't dare waste any time. There was only one way to get out of these mountains, and that was to keep heading west – no telling how far. When the panic threatened to come again, however, he put it down and washed his face and hands, then made himself leave the little stream.

The sun went behind the mountains early, but there was still plenty of light in the sky above, so he kept going until it finally got too dark to find his footing. He thought of going on by moonlight, but he was trembling with weariness. When he came to another brook, he decided it was wiser to stop and try to get a little sleep. Behind some rocks he found a sheltered place where the pine needles had piled in deep, and lay down with the Mackinaw over him, more for comfort than for warmth. The night was fine and clear, and the coolness had no bite in it.

As he lay there looking up at the stars almost drowned out in the moon brilliance, the forests seemed quieter than the night before. Or maybe the little night sounds were covered over by the near-by bubble of the stream. Barney thought, almost dispassionately, about the emptiness of his belly. An odd new feeling settled over him, a dried-out anger that had to do with all he knew of people, and with the luck that seemed to run away from the good ones and favour the bad ones. He thought of Steve, but tried not to, because it was too late to help him now, and what, after all, could anybody do against a man like Doc and all the people who were willing to believe him? And yet he had to think of Steve – the blunt misery was part of this strange cold, tearless, feeling. His father was part of it, too. All the inevitability of death – even his own death – suddenly became believable and acceptable to him. He even was able to tell the real nature of this new way of looking at things. Barney felt old.

The night seemed to go on a long time, and at the first broadening of light in the sky he got up. Washing himself in the little brook, he took another long drink, to fill the emptiness in his belly. As he squatted down there beside the stream, the sun found a notch in the hills and reached down to lay a coating of sudden warmth over his shoulders. Swinging round to take a hard look, Barney could hardly believe his eyes. For the sun was coming from behind and the brook was falling away ahead of him, draining westward. Somehow, in the last part of the evening before, he'd come across the divide and was on his way down. All he'd have to do now was to follow the stream far enough and he'd reach the floor of the next valley, unless his legs gave out.

He stood up and headed off downhill, setting himself to watch for anything that might serve for food. As he crossed an open clearing in the woods, a soft lap of grass between the rocky lanes of the mountain sides, he found a stand of young dandelions. They hadn't begun to bud or turn bitter, and the heart and stalks were sweet and crisp. He ate quite a few, hoping they'd keep him going, though they didn't drive off his hunger.

His real find came late that afternoon when he was taking drinks from the stream every ten minutes or so to keep his belly from grinding. As he followed the little freshet through a stand of bushes, he raised a grouse hen, and it occurred to him that the bird must have got off a nest somewhere near. After ten minutes of picking through the brush, he found it. The sight of the eight eggs in it made his hunger come to the surface all in a rush, and he had to warn himself that they might not be new-laid – if they were just ready to hatch, he was in for a disappointment. But the first one he broke was as fresh as if it had come from the nest of one of Aunt Norah's laying hens, and so were the others. If anyone had told Barney before this that he'd take such a pleasure in raw eggs, he'd have laughed out loud. As it was, he thought he'd never eaten anything so welcome.

With his energies revived, he made good time going down the mountain for the next hour or so. He lost the sun as he followed the brook down a tortuous little canyon. Then, all at once, he came out into it again and found himself through the deep part of the range, standing on a brow of rock just above the foothills. Beyond, out under the long dusty yellow rays of the late afternoon light, stretching away westward was a flat plain. On the far side of it rose a big hill – not exactly a mountain but a high lumpy mound, the sort of hill which Uncle George called a butte. And at the foot of it, where it levelled off on to the flat, there curved a stream, glittering in the late sun – just like a long silver bow.

20

BARNEY smelled the bacon from quite a way off. When he got closer, he knew there were beans cooking too. He looked at the flapping tent, the scrawny team of horses grazing near by, the big rocky hole in the ground and the man squatted beside his campfire. Intently, he walked straight over.

The man looked up, level-eyed and unsmiling.

Barney said, 'Do you have any chores I could do to earn some food?'

The man studied him silently, looked past him across the flat towards the mountains from which he'd come. 'If you're hungry, set and eat.'

Barney sat down on a stone, took the tin plate that was handed him and attacked the meal with single-minded relish. The man watched thoughtfully, ate some of his own ration, then leaned forward and threw another slab of bacon into the pan.

When he'd finished that too and a mess of fried dough, Barney looked up gratefully. 'Thank you for the breakfast, sir.' And though he was itching to be on his way again, he added. 'I'd like to help you clean up.'

'Then do,' said the man.

While Barney scoured the plates in the stream, the man sat and watched with a look that Uncle George would have called 'poker-faced'. Barney thought that this was all right with him – after all the made-to-order smiles that had been put on around him lately, it was even restful. When he had done what he could think of to pay for his meal, he came back.

'I guess I'll be going. Thanks again.'

The man stood up and stretched. 'Ain't none of my business where you're headin',' he drawled, 'but if it happened t'be Butte, y'could ride with me. I'm drivin' that way this morning.'

Barney couldn't help but think back to the last time he'd accepted a ride, but there were no strings attached this time, and he could see no danger in it. Together they went to hitch the sorry team to the wagon, which he now saw was full of rock from the diggings.

'Low-grade ore,' explained the man, following his look. 'Ain't hardly worth cartin' in.' And as they backed the team into place, he added, 'Hard on hosses, haulin' rock.'

They drove across the grassy flat two hours or more. Finally they reached the river, which was shallow enough to ford almost anywhere, and headed up towards the dry-looking hill with its ramshackle jerry-built town sprawling along its steep slopes. It reminded Barney of the lower part of Alder Gulch, and the nearer they got, the more discouraged he felt. It seemed another unlikely place to find his father.

Out of the silence that had stretched over the miles, the man beside him suddenly spoke up. 'You're a quiet one, for so young. Most kids always chatterin'. Good thing for a boy to learn to keep his mouth shut.' And having pronounced that, he clamped his own closed in a straight line.

Barney wondered at it a little himself. A lag in the conversation used to make him uncomfortable, even prompted him to do a lot of useless talking to fill it up. Now he was glad enough to leave it alone.

'Well, I could ask you a question,' he admitted finally.

'Then do it.'

'If you were looking for a man who might be in that town, where would you ask first?'

'Assay office,' said the miner. 'Any man comes here is lookin' for black-ledge. If he finds it, he's got to have it assayed, see how much silver she's runnin'. Assayer keeps records.'

And after a while Barney asked once more. 'Is this a good town to live in?'

'No, it ain't. It's a bearcat.'

Since that was all that passed between them, it was odd that Barney felt a twinge of regret as he stepped out of the wagon in front of the Wells Fargo building. The man stared down at him a minute and nodded. Barney gave him a sort of half-salute, a gesture that came natural to him, though he didn't think he'd ever done it before. He had to stop and remember where he'd learned it, and then realized it was a manner his father had of saying 'thanks' and 'good-bye' at the same time.

As he walked in under the sign that said ASSAYER, he braced himself for another failure. Without any real hope that he'd get an answer, he asked the man behind the cage if they had a John Morgan on their records. The clerk ruffled through some papers in a drawer, finally turned up what he was looking for and eyed Barney over the top of his spectacles.

'All we've got is "Morgan". If you want to find out his first name, you can go out to Walkerville and ask him yourself. He's got a claim about four miles north of here – the "Misfortune".' With that he shut the drawer.

Footsore as he was, Barney couldn't help thinking that four miles was a long way to go just to get disappointed all over again. But maybe this Morgan would know if there were any others around. He was fairly sure it couldn't be his father – it wouldn't be John Morgan's way, to give a mine a downhearted name.

And yet, as he headed out along the dusty road north, Barney discovered that his weariness went only so far now. It was as if his trip through the mountains had given him some sort of say-so over his body, so that it couldn't tell him any more that it wouldn't go on. When his legs began to ache and sweat ran down his face, he hardly thought about it, but kept slogging along. He wouldn't even sit down and rest. Rest didn't get you anywhere, he decided, and time had a way of going on ahead while you sat still.

It was late afternoon when he happened to pass a claim where a couple of miners were loading ore into a wagon and stopped to ask directions. One of them thought the Misfortune was west, on the road to Rocker, but the other argued him down.

'Na-a-a, you're thinkin' of the Mischance. The Misfortune is that one-man diggin's about a mile north of here. . . .'

Barney left them still jawing at each other and went on. It was a half-hour later and the sun was almost down when he came to the battered old sign hanging crooked on its stake, but he could read the weather-beaten lettering. A hundred feet along a path he came to a shaft, a six-foot-square rough hole in the ground that fell away deep, out of sight. On one edge of it was a windlass with a long arm, for hauling up the ore, and beyond that was a pile of fresh-cut rock. Built on to one wall of the hole, leading down into the dimness below, was a ladder, a workmanly job with square well-made joints.

As he stood there, Barney heard someone climbing up it, saw a man with a lantern. He was covered with rock dust from head to foot – it crusted his lean face and stood thick on his dark hair – but as he stepped up out of the hole and his eyes met Barney's, they knew each other almost at the same instant.

It wasn't exactly as Barney had pictured it. There wasn't any jumping and shouting and questions and explanations. John Morgan set down the lantern and walked over, blinking as if he thought the dust in his eyes might be playing him tricks. With his hands on Barney's shoulders, he took light hold of the boy as if testing his realness. There was just an instant of awkward silence.

Then Barney said, 'I had a hard time finding you.'

And the size of that understatement struck him so that he had to laugh. Which made his father laugh too. And the years of being separated were brushed away in the warm sound of the two of them laughing, together.

'I wrote you after I left Virginia City,' John Morgan said. 'The letter must have miscarried. And it wasn't two weeks ago that I sent George another bank draft to pay for your keep. I'll admit it was the first I've been able to send in a long time, but before I left Virginia I mailed him money regular. He had no right to try to send you back east without telling me.'

'Then you're not mad at me for running away?'

'Of course not, though I'm sorry it had to be done that way. I see now that I should have come back for you, but I . . .' He smiled a little ruefully. 'I hated to come back empty-handed. And I didn't think this was any sort of place for a boy.' He glanced round at the tent.

It was night and they were sitting in front of a small make-shift stove with a little fire going to keep off the chill. Barney thought he'd hardly ever been so comfortable, with a ration of jerky and brown bread in his belly and his feet stretched out beside his dad's near the fire. His father was looking at him wonderingly, as if he could still hardly believe what he saw.

'I reckon I forgot how you were growing, all the time I was gone. If you were able to make it all the way here, alone on foot from the ranch, you can take whatever life I lead.' There was a pride and satisfaction in the way he said it that finished off any lingering doubts Barney might have had about the rightness of his coming.

'I wasn't exactly alone all the way,' he admitted. As he told his story, there were parts he would rather have left out – about how he'd thought Doc so clever at first, and how he'd once given Steve a punch. But he told it straight through down to the last detail, while his father listened quietly, frowning once in a while, especially when Barney came to where Doc had drawn up the counterfeit papers.

'That man must be a real bad 'un,' he murmured.

And when Barney told about giving the nugget to Billy, his father nodded sharply. 'You did exactly right.'

Finally, after he'd told about the trek through the mountains alone and how he'd finally found the bird's eggs, John Morgan looked at him, silent and searching.

'Seems like you've learned a deal of horse sense along the way somewhere,' he said.

'Well, I remembered a lot from the days you took me out walking when we were back east together. It was you that told me about snow water and the north side of hills. . . .'

'I did?'

Barney nodded. 'But I wouldn't have got here, I'll bet, if it wasn't for Steve.' And the worry that had been rankling at the back of his mind all this while began to get more acute as he spoke it out loud. 'I'm scared for him, Dad!'

'I was just thinking the same thing,' agreed his father. 'I reckon it's up to us to get him away from that outfit.'

'But how? We don't even have a gun!'

'And if we did, we might have to shoot somebody with it. Which would mean we'd have to set ourselves up as judge and jury and executioner, and that's more than I ever felt I had the right to do.'

'But you said yourself, Doc's a bad man.'

'I believe your friend Steve would agree with me when I say that there's only one way to stop this doctor fellow, and that's to out-think him.'

'But how?'

'Some things you can't figure ahead of time,' said John Morgan thoughtfully. 'Just have to play the cards as they're dealt.'

21

ALL the way into town that next afternoon, Barney's father talked along, more than the boy had ever heard him speak in the old days at home. Of course, there was a lot to tell – how he'd had to sell his horse to pay for the mine and that was why they had to walk to town, and how the mine wasn't bringing much return – things like that, which had nothing to do with the job they had to do. Barney figured that his father was trying to keep their minds off the trouble they were heading into.

Once they got to town, though, he was all business. It wasn't hard to find where Doc's Miracle Show was set up – just about everybody was talking about it. It was the first travelling entertainment that had come to Butte, and the men were fairly starved for it. That made Barney uneasy; it seemed to him they were in for a hard time if just the two of them had to take on Doc and the miners, too. But he kept it to himself as he and John Morgan walked out south of town near enough to see the camp. As he pointed out each of the wagons, it gave Barney a strange feeling to watch Maddie and Billy going on about their chores while Hoke snoozed as usual, tipped back on his stool against his wagon, the bullwhip looped on his belly.

His father made him go over again all the details he could remember of how the Show worked and what Doc usually said and how he tricked people.

'They thought he was wonderful in Virginia City,' added the boy bitterly.

'Don't try to compare that with this,' his father told him. 'Butte's made of different stuff. Folks here are hard-rock miners, not saddle tramps like the panners down in Alder Gulch, but neither are they money-grubbing bankers and businessmen. They like a good time, but they're really here to work. Every man of them's got a stake in this town and is hanging on to it against long odds. You see, there never was much gold here, and what little was got scraped up quick. The town almost died out, but a few people knew something about quartz and they knew there was silver if a man was willing to dig for it. It's taken time, but the town has come back these last few years since they got a mill to grind up the ore. Even so, it's still not easy money. The ore doesn't mill well. What we need is a smelter, but there's no money for that. So we make out the best we can. If I keep at it from sun-up to dark, I make enough to buy beans. That's the way a lot of men are doing it here. So, as I say, they're a fairly stubborn, hard-headed bunch that won't take to being slick-talked out of their money – not if it can be proved to 'em.'

They ate an early supper that night at a cheap restaurant near the edge of town and were back at the camping ground when the calliope gave forth its opening blast. All through the first Show John Morgan stood and listened.

The bally was changed somewhat. Billy's juggling act still came first, then Suzette did a couple of tricks, after which Hoke introduced Doc, who went right into his talk about the Curative. When he'd sold a half-dozen bottles, he invited the crowd into the tent to witness the great mind-reading abilities of Madame Medea. Not a word about the strongest man in the world. All on tenterhooks, Barney looked at his father.

John Morgan just stood quiet, hands in his pockets, the flat-crowned black hat pulled low over his eyes and a brooding calculation in his look. Finally, as the juggling act ended the second time, he glanced down at Barney.

'You stay here, Buz. Don't try to wade in and help, no matter what happens. I don't want you to get hurt, and I don't want to be worried about you.'

Unbuttoning his old denim coat, he set it back on his shoulders so that it seemed not to fit very well. With his thumb he shoved his hat back on his head so that some of his hair came loose in front. Reaching down, he snapped off the top of a piece of grass and stuck it between his teeth, hooked his thumbs into his belt, and strolled forward through the crowd, looking for all the world like the sleepiest rube that ever hit town.

Barney stood and watched, all edges inside. He kept scanning the faces of the men round him, trying to see the stoutness in them that would back his father up if the need came. At least they weren't got up in fancy clothes and there weren't any laced-up ladies around.

Now, as the calliope died down, Doc stepped forward unannounced, since Hoke was still in the tent with the first crowd, and began to hand out his pamphlets. As he started to talk about the wonderful ingredients of the Curative, Barney heard his father speak up, not as brisk as usual, but with a lazy sort of drawl.

'You got some of that stuff for sale, doctor?' he called from the front of the crowd.

Doc explained about not having many bottles left, but was quick enough to go in the tent and bring a few out. He passed one down to Barney's father, who uncorked it and took a healthy drink, while the rest of the audience watched.

Somebody hollered, 'What's it taste like?'

'Can't tell,' hollered back John Morgan, loud enough for

them all to hear. 'There's so tarnation much red pepper in it, I can't get through to the real taste. What's all the red pepper supposed to cure, doctor?'

The crowd got still, listening for Doc's reply. He was smooth about it, too. 'That's not pepper, my friend,' he said pleasantly. 'That's a rare essence distilled from –'

Morgan interrupted him. 'From these here grasses along the Siberian steppes, like it says in your handbill here?'

'Exactly. I've conducted experiments to –'

'I don't believe it.' Morgan looked round at the rest of the crowd. 'If grass ever tasted like that, a self-respectin' hoss wouldn't touch it. What's more, I don't think this whole crowd is sufferin' from all that weakness you mention here in your paper. I think you're pushin' your luck, doctor, comin' to a workin'-man's town like this and tryin' to sell us on bein' sick. This whole thing –' he waved the pamphlet – 'sounds like a made-up piece of foolery. I'll lay anybody here ten to one I can prove it, too! Anybody want to bet with me?'

He got several takers, and some in the crowd began to make side bets while Doc called out, 'Gentlemen! Gentlemen!' but nobody listened to him. He walked up and down impatiently.

'Put up your money,' shouted John Morgan, 'and I'll put mine with it and then I'm goin' to ask this doctor-fellow one question. If he won't answer, the bet's off.'

The crowd was keen for it, and Doc, frowning slightly, seemed nervous for the first time since Barney had known him.

'Come, come, my man,' he cried impatiently, his voice rising over the chatter of the crowd. 'Clear out of here with your gambling. You're interfering with charitable work!'

'I'm not interfering with a blamed thing,' asserted Morgan. 'I'm helpin' you, doctor. Here's your chance to prove to these people that you really know what you're talkin' about – if you do, which I doubt. This paper says you came out here to cure us of some weakness brought on by locoweed poisonin'. All I say is, if you're an expert on it, you won't be afraid to answer me one question.'

There was such a racket of insistence that Doc couldn't do anything but agree. 'Then make it brief,' he said coldly. 'There are sufferers in this crowd who need my help.'

'So you say. What *I* say is, locoweed never hurt anybody unless they ate it. Of course, we've all seen what it does to cattle – isn't a man here doesn't know that. As for its flower dust, I don't know, and I don't think you know. Doctor, I'm bettin' you don't even know what *colour* the flower is!'

The crowd got suddenly so quiet you could hear the flutter of the kerosene flares up round the platform. Doc looked a little sickly in the uneven light. 'The many species of the plant are ... There are far more varieties of locoweed than most people realize ...' he began.

Their hoots drowned him out.

'We're talkin' about the Montana kind,' Morgan told him. 'We all know what it looks like. Do you?'

And then Doc made his big mistake. He guessed. 'Well, of course this is the yellow –'

A shout of laughter rose.

'– yellow-rooted variety,' he went on desperately, 'but the blossoms are ... red.'

And now the crowd did howl, because there wasn't a man among them who wasn't familiar with the little blue-purple flowers out on the range. Loud yells of 'Fake' and 'Bunko' and 'Sharper' began to come thick and fast.

Doc made one last desperate try. With all the hauteur at his command, he stared down at them sombrely and said, 'If you will have the mercy to quieten yourselves, you'll do this poor man a kindness.' He pointed at John Morgan. 'He does not know it, but, as a doctor, I can assure you that he is dangerously ill. I've been trying to humour him, since the least agitation may actually cause a tragedy right here in our midst!'

He spoke with such terrible grimness that the crowd almost got its attention turned for a minute. As they crowded in to see who he was talking about, their clamour fell away to a full-throated burr of doubts and suspicion.

'Can you prove that?' Morgan demanded. 'We're a hard-headed bunch up here, doctor. We can take the truth, but we want to see it proved. I say I'm as healthy as you and a sight more honest. I say it's the worst deceit a man can work, to try to put the fear of sickness into people's minds. Come on, doctor, play your cards. I'm callin' you.'

Once more the miners grew silent as Doc invited Morgan up on to the platform and called for the glass of water.

'Now, then, my friend –' he handed the water over – 'breathe through this,' and from his inside vest pocket he produced the metal tube, just as he had done before.

'Tell you what.' John Morgan grinned. 'Before I do that, suppose you stir this water around with the end of that blow-stick just to make sure there's nothin' fixed to the end of it to colour up the water.'

For a second Doc went dead-still. Then, in a thin voice that Barney recognized and still shivered from, he said, 'Poor fellow, you're sicker than I thought. Just wait here a moment, please.' Stepping to the door of the tent, he pulled back the flap and called one word, as if he were calling someone's name.

'Clem!'

Then he returned to face John Morgan. 'Young man, I'd be curious to know why you want to spend these last precious days of yours in such scepticism. I only came here trying to help you and your friends out there. I haven't asked for your money, have I? My services are free. . . .'

'They weren't free to that bunch that went into the tent just now. I saw you pick up thirty-forty dollars from 'em, and money like that comes hard these days. Give me the blow-pipe.' Before Doc could stop him, Morgan reached out, got the pipette and stirred the water, holding it up so that the crowd could watch it turn red. 'A cheap magician's trick. A few bottles of pepper water and a lot of free hot air.' He turned to Doc. 'Mister, you are worse than a quack doctor, you are a thief!'

The crowd surged forward as if at some signal. Picks and fists and whisky bottles were being swung about. Barney couldn't see over the confusion, had to scramble to keep from being trampled on. Deciding his father had plenty of help, he dodged and skirted round the edge of the mêlée, making a wide circle to come up behind the tent. He was heading for Steve's wagon when he almost ran into the crowd of people that Maddie was hustling out of the back exit of the tent, much to their evident bewilderment.

Barney knew she saw him – she ducked back over towards her own wagon – but he didn't care. He was too busy trying to fight his way over to Steve's door. Then, all at once, she was back, facing him, and he was looking straight into the ugly double snout of a shotgun. In the flickering light of the lanterns Maddie's eyes were colder than frozen dirty water.

'You tipped the crowd, didn't you, you scrawny brat! You done this!'

Barney was watching her thumb as it cocked first one ham-mer, then the other. Though he couldn't take his eyes off her hands, he sensed someone off to one side in the shadows. There was a quick movement, and something spun in an arc across the darkness. Maddie's yelp of pain was drowned out by the shattering roar of the shotgun. There was a hot streak across his left arm, but Barney realized, in a daze, that the full force of the blast had missed him, scattering harmlessly into the ground a few feet away.

And now men were running to them, they had Maddie and were holding her, but Barney was looking at Billy. The coloured boy walked across and carefully picked up the Indian club he had thrown to break Maddie's aim.

Barney's father was by his side now, looking at the arm anxiously, upset for the first time that night.

'Thank the good Lord,' he said fervently. 'You only got grazed by one piece of shot.'

Slowly as a dream it came over the boy that the reason he was seeing all this so clearly was that a new weird light was playing over the scene, the raging reddish glare of fire.

'It's – burning,' he said woodenly.

'Like a haystack. The whole works is going to go. That fat fellow with the whip took a slice at me, and I ducked. The whip caught on one of the torches and knocked it into the tent.'

All the gold seals and red ribbons – burning. All the papers and banners and bottles. Barney wished Steve could – Steve! He was jolted out of the shock he'd been in ever since the shotgun blast. Turning feverishly, he found that his father was ahead of him, inspecting the door and padlock.

'If only I had a pick . . .' He frowned.

And then from inside came the welcomest sound Barney had ever heard. In a quiet steady voice that reached them clearly through the panels, Steve called, 'Stand out of the way. I can break it down.'

Morgan shook his head doubtfully, but stepped back. 'Go ahead. You're clear.'

Twice the strong man threw his weight against the door. The second time, the lock bent and the wood around the hinges splintered loose. The third time, the panels seemed to burst at the seams as Steve half fell through.

And it was all over.

22

LATE that next afternoon, as they sat around at the mine, Steve told them what had gone on after he'd got taken back. The strong man looked a good deal different, clean-shaven and with his hair cut, young and as keen of face as John Morgan. The two men had hit it off like good friends right from the beginning.

For the first time Steve didn't sound disgusted and bitter when he talked. '. . . so Doc wasn't sure whether I meant it or not when I told him I'd never work for him again. The stubborner I got, the more he talked, still trying to hold his threats over my head. But the showdown never came, because when he kicked the knife out of my hand that night, he dislocated a bone in my wrist and I couldn't go on with my act anyhow. There was nothing he could do but wait and see whether I intended to stick by my words or not.'

'But as soon as your wrist was well,' Barney said, 'you'd have – he'd have – What would have happened?'

Steve shrugged. 'I guess I'd have found out whether he was bluffing.'

Barney's father cut in then. 'No use supposing what might have happened. The main thing is, they're gone now – left on the stage for St Louis this morning, and I'd say it'll be a long time before they're in a position to swindle anybody again. They lost everything in the fire except the clothes they had on. Even had to sell their teams to a dealer to get the money to go back east. The horses will be put up at auction tomorrow. I'm fair tempted to buy one myself, but I thought I ought to put it to the rest of the partnership first. It all depends on what we decide we do.'

He looked around at them, sitting on the ground in a circle – Steve like a contented giant, his long legs crossed under him, elbows on his knees, the bandage on his right wrist white against his swarthy skin; Billy on the other side of him, diffident and shy, but with a new soft shine to his face as if he knew he had a good right to be part of their circle; then Barney.

'I'll draw you the picture so you can all help to decide,' John Morgan said. 'Here we've got a mine. It isn't a very good one – one man alone can't dig enough silver to make it really worth while. Four of us might if we live cheap. If I could stay down in the hole and bust rock, and Steve could haul it up, and the boys do the chores around camp, we'd make out, but we wouldn't get rich. The thing to consider is the future. Everybody says the silver's petering out in most of the mines. Fellow that owns the Anaconda is down near three hundred feet, and he says he's just about through. I'm only down a little over a hundred, and my ore is getting so full of copper, I'm having trouble selling it.'

'Copper?' Barney tried to think what he'd heard about copper.

'Yes, and a nuisance it is. Makes the ore so refractory it doesn't yield to the milling process.'

'What's the choice?' asked Steve.

'To sell. Man came out last week and made me an offer – not much, but at least it was cash.'

'What will he do with it if you can't make a living off it?'

'I asked him that very question. He told me he's got machinery at another mine near here where the lode has given out. Says he's willing to cart his equipment over and clean up what's left of this one. With machinery, he says he could dig enough to make a fair profit.'

'I know!' It broke out of Barney suddenly, as he remembered. 'I know what I heard about copper.' He told them what the Western Union men had said about the telegraph wires having to be of copper. 'They said there were going to be lines all over the country someday. Why couldn't copper be a good thing to mine?'

Thoughtfully his father said, 'Isn't worth much now, nobody here puts any store by it. Newspaper printed a front-page story not long ago, said Butte was all finished, be a ghost town inside a year.'

'Newspapers', blurted Barney, 'are written by ordinary people like me – and sometimes not even honest ones.' He sounded so suspicious that his father grinned and Steve laughed approvingly.

'I go along with Barney,' Steve said. 'Printed words can be used as a trap.'

John Morgan nodded. 'I wondered whether maybe somebody wasn't trying to scare us small mine-owners out and buy up our holdings cheap. Couldn't figure out why, but maybe Barney's hit it. Maybe it's copper. There's a lot of it down there – it's deep, but it's rich. Some of the assays around here run higher than seventy-five per cent copper. If it ever gets worth a price, whoever owns a piece of this hill will get rich.'

'I vote we stay!' shouted Barney, his eyes shining.

'If we do, it'll mean work and expense. We'll have to buy a team and a wagon to cart the ore to town. Paying somebody to do that has eaten up a lot of my profits.'

Billy spoke up now timidly. 'I got this here old nugget. Would that buy a horse?'

Morgan took the piece of gold, weighed it in his hand. 'It would buy two.'

'And if it's work you need, I'm your man,' said Steve.

'Then I guess it's unanimous.' Barney's father looked pleased. 'I'll admit, I hated the thought of leaving the old Misfortune. I've taken a fancy to her.'

'The what?' asked Steve.

Barney spoke up, too. 'Why did you name her that, Dad?'

His father looked surprised. 'Matter of fact, I didn't. Fellow I bought it from tacked that name on to her – Come to think of it, it doesn't have a very lucky sound. If I had a can of paint, I'd change it this minute.'

'Stoveblack works pretty good,' suggested Barney. He went to collect some from the stove while Morgan walked out to the road and wrenched the sign off its loose fastenings to bring it back. With one swipe of the black stuff, he crossed out the letters MIS.

'There,' he said. 'The claim is now named the FORTUNE – and a proper name it is.'

'I'll put it up,' Barney offered. He got the hammer and nails and took the sign out to the road. With a few strokes he had it in place – straight and sound this time.

For a minute he eyed it, taking satisfaction in the thought of the work to come and the partners who'd be sharing it. As he turned to go back to them, with the late yellow sunlight streaming ahead of him, Barney was thinking that even a light-built man can cast a tall shadow.

In case the reader may wonder whether Barney's hunch paid off – within two years, the railroad came in to Montana, copper boomed, and the big butte became known as 'the richest hill on earth'.

*Some other Puffin Books
are described on the
following pages*

CHILDREN ON THE OREGON TRAIL

A. Rutgers van der Loeff

This book, by the author of *Avalanche!*, is based on the true life-story of thirteen-year-old John Sager, who, with his family, was part of a covered-wagon band of settlers who set out for the Far West of America in the summer of 1844.

His parents died on the journey and the other pioneers decided to turn off and take the easier way to California, but John with his six younger brothers and sisters left the safety of the wagon train to keep faith with his father's dream of opening up the West for American settlers. Together the children made the almost unbelievable journey across two rivers, through hostile Indian territory, and over the Cascade Mountains.

The story of the appalling hardships which they endured – and of the outcome of their courage – can be read in this magnificently written tale, which we believe to be one of the most spellbinding ever published in Puffins. Noel Streatfeild, who chose it as an *Elizabethan* Book of the Month, called it 'a classic story which I for one will never forget'.

Especially for boys over ten, but also for girls who enjoy robust adventure.

SONGBERD'S GROVE

Anne Barrett

When Martin Singer, with his mother and father, moves into his new home at No. 7 Songberd's Grove, he is depressed by the shabby and neglected street. Then he discovers that it is dominated by a big bully, called Lennie, who has made all the other children so frightened of him that they do whatever he says, and he *likes* it to be dirty. Martin refuses to join his 'gang' so he smashes his milk bottles and spoils his garden.

The grown-ups in the street know nothing about this and when Mr Singer repaints their front door Martin and his upstairs neighbour, a tough little girl called Geneva, realize they've got to protect it, so they start a two-man revolt. How they succeed both in vanquishing the bully and making the street beautiful and famous all adds up to a thoroughly exciting story.

For boys and girls of 10 years and over.